DARK SECRETS

THE SHADOW GUILD BOOK 3

LINSEY HALL

CARROW

I stepped back and looked up, admiring the sign we'd just hung.

CARROW BURTON: SUPERNATURAL SLEUTH

"I don't know." Mac crossed her arms and frowned up at the sign. "I think maybe we should have gone with 'Supernatural Scooby.'"

I laughed. "I didn't know you were a father."

"What?"

"That was a total dad joke."

Mac shrugged. "He's really got a nose for crimes."

I turned back to admire the placard hanging over the green door that led up to our flats. The black and white wooden sign was a gift from my friends Mac, Eve, and Quinn. It was my first day as a real live magical mystery solver in Guild City. Exciting.

A faint breeze blew my hair back, and the sun struggled to peep out from behind the clouds. It was another rainy day in London, which meant that Guild City was getting damp, too. Our hidden town experienced all the same weather as London, and the day was miserable.

"Thanks for the sign," I said, smiling at Mac.

"When will you register with the Council?" she asked.

The Council of Guilds was the official government of my new city. As a new business, I'd need to register with them.

"I don't know."

I wasn't yet a member of a guild, and the Council did *not* like that. My new enterprise should be protected under the umbrella of one of the dozen guilds in the city. Unfortunately, none of them would have me because no one really knew what species I was, including me.

Hence the somewhat ambiguous designation *Supernatural Sleuth* on the sign, since I wasn't technically a witch or a seer.

Maybe I shouldn't open my new business without the protection of a guild, a move that was bound to gain the eye of the Council, but I needed money to pay the rent, so...

It was a risk I was willing to take.

"Hello?" A tremulous voice sounded from behind me. "Are you open for business?"

A potential customer!

Pleasure shot through me.

I turned and spotted a beautiful woman standing about ten feet away. She was clutching a book, and her gaze went from the sign to me. She had long dark hair and brilliant green eyes, and though she appeared scared out of her wits, she radiated strength. It was in the straightness of her spine and the intensity of her gaze.

"I am." I didn't reach my hand out to shake hers, since my power might allow me to read information about her. I preferred to do that only with permission. "I'm Carrow Burton."

"Seraphia." She gave a little wave. I spotted a flash of pale light against her wrist, the luminous tattoo of a leaf or vine, then it was gone.

"How can I help you?" I asked.

She held up the book, a battered leather volume that pulsed with magic. "I work at the library, and I need help with this book."

"Oh, aren't you the upstairs librarian?" Mac said.

"Yes, precisely."

"Not my area, but it's cool up there." Mac shot me a look. "I'm more of a murder mystery kind of girl, but Seraphia here works in the history section of the library."

"History of where?" I asked, interest piqued. "Guild City?"

"A bit, yes," said Seraphia. "But also history of the magical communities throughout the world. So my department includes spell books and hexanaries, things like that."

"Hexanaries?"

"Like dictionaries of hexes."

"Ah." Thunder rumbled in the distance, and I shot a look at the sky. Roiling black clouds crept toward us. "We'd better get inside." I grimaced. "You can tell me more about your problem once we're out of this weather."

Seraphia nodded. "Thank you."

The first fat raindrops fell, one of them splashing right on my forehead. Mac, who was closest to the entrance, darted inside.

I gestured for Seraphia to follow. "Go on, Mac will lead you up."

She hurried through the green door. I gave my new sign one last admiring look, then entered the building and shut the door behind us. Mac took the stairs two at a time toward my top-floor flat with Seraphia in the rear. I climbed the steps after them, passing Mac's door. It was ajar. Through the opening, I spied my raccoon familiar, Cordelia, digging through Mac's kitchen cupboards.

"No!" I pointed at her. "Inside manners."

Cordelia glared at me but withdrew her little hand from the packet of crisps into which she was digging.

"I'm watching you," I said.

She glared harder.

"Leave her be," Mac shouted from the little landing outside my door. "She's fine."

"She'll eat all your crisps and biscuits," I warned. "It's why she's at your place instead of mine. She's already nicked the good stuff out of my cupboards."

"I like the company," Mac said.

I shrugged and climbed the last flight to my door. As I stepped onto the landing, an invisible hand seemed to grasp my insides and twist. Pain shot through me, and I gasped, doubling over.

"Carrow!" Mac gripped my arm, keeping me upright. "What's wrong?"

Cold sweat popped out on my brow, and I struggled to breathe through the nausea.

"Are you all right?" Seraphia's voice echoed with concern.

"I'm . . . fine." I struggled to straighten, my insides still churning.

"Your signature..." Her voice trailed off. "It's changed."

"Changed?" *Oh, no. Not again.*

"Your eyes..." Mac frowned. "They're glowing green. They looked the same way after you absorbed the magic in Orion's Heart."

I'd saved Guild City, but I'd been infused with dark necromancer magic in the process. Magic that I had no idea what to do with.

Magic that was screwing me up inside.

The pain subsided, and I regained control of my breathing.

"You look better," Seraphia said. "But are you sure there isn't anything I can do for you?"

"Don't worry about me. It's a little thing." I tried to give her a reassuring smile, but she just stared at me, concern still creasing her brow. I gestured to my door, which was open. "Go on. We'll sort out this book of yours."

"All right." She entered my flat, an aura of worry radiating around her.

I looked at Mac. "Are my eyes still weird?"

"It's faded now, but..."

"We need to figure this out." I shook my head. "Whatever it is."

Please don't turn me evil.

I could feel the newness of the magical world right now—my almost complete unfamiliarity with it. Was it even possible to turn evil?

Mac squeezed my arm. "We'll get to the bottom of it."

"Yeah. But first, I've got to get my Scooby on."

She grinned and followed me into my flat. The little space was decorated with the eclectic assortment of furniture that she, Eve, and Quinn had found in the secondhand shop down the street. It was all different styles and colors, accented with portraits of colorful animals, but I liked the crazy.

It went well with the ancient, sloping floor and low ceiling. A little window looked out over the street, and it felt like living in a slice of the past that had been combined with a cozy present. Far better than my cold, lonely flat in the dodgy part of London.

I met Seraphia's gaze and gestured to the couch. "Have a seat. Would you like a cup of tea?"

Seraphia thrust the book at me. "No. I want you to look at this."

"Sure." I gestured to the small, round table in the corner that served as my dining area. "You can put it there."

I didn't want to touch it until I knew the nature of her problem. The last thing I needed was to be hit by an unexpected vision. Or worse, one over which I had no power. I still didn't have a lot of control over my magic, but I was getting better.

Seraphia set the book on the table. Her shoulders relaxed, as though she was rid of an unsavory burden. She turned to me. "I'm sorry to be so abrupt, but this problem..."

"Is bigger than a cup of tea?" Mac asked.

"Exactly."

"Tell me about it." I took a seat on the couch, my legs still a bit wobbly from earlier.

She sat on the other side, and Seraphia took the cushy armchair in the corner.

"I work at the library, as I told you," Seraphia said. "It's a quiet life. Mostly taking care of the collection and answering questions. And we *do* have some dangerous books, like the hexanaries I mentioned. But mostly it's just me and the stacks. Nothing ever happens."

"Until that book happened." I looked at it, my curiosity rising. "What's it called?"

"*A Most Elucidating History of Guild City*. I've never read it. Didn't even know it was in the collection, in fact. Until I felt it. This dark magic signature..."

"It came from the book?" I looked at the tome, unable to sense anything from that far away.

"Exactly. It's faded now, but it's still there if I touch it." Confusion flickered in her eyes. "Some pages were torn out."

"Recently?"

"I don't know. Could have been a long time ago."

"Anything else you should tell me before I handle it?"

She shook her head. "Just that it felt like death itself when I touched it the first time. Like it was trying to tear my heart straight out of my chest."

I winced.

"Exactly." She nodded. "It was terrible. I've never felt anything like it, which is why I wanted you to look at it."

"Why me and not a seer?"

"I've heard how you saved Guild City, and you seemed like the perfect person for the job."

"Well, hopefully, I can figure out what's wrong with your book." My mind flashed to payment. It was a normal businessperson thing, to ask for money for a service rendered. It was half the reason I'd started this business, in fact. I needed to be paid for my work if I wanted to stay on top of my rent. But how did one ask for payment from someone who is in trouble?

As if she could read my thoughts, she asked. "What is your fee?"

"I suppose that depends on who is paying." I'd charge the Devil of Darkvale—Grey, as I now thought of him—a hell of a lot more because he was rich as Croesus. But someone who didn't have a lot of money? I'd charge them less.

"I can afford it," Seraphia said. "Or at the very least, the library can. The book is from their collection, after all."

"Then we'll work it out after the fact."

I rose and strode over to the book.

My skin prickled with awareness at the slight pulse of dark magic coming from the leather and paper.

"You might want to sit," Seraphia said. "First time I touched it, I fell on my arse."

I took her advice and slid into a chair, feeling their gazes on me. I drew in a breath, focusing on the object in front of me and on the magic welling inside me.

Control.

I needed to see what *I* wanted to see. Not whatever blasted out at me.

I looked at Seraphia. "What do you most want to know about this book and its dark magic?"

"Why now? It's been in the collection for years, I think. So why is it now saturated in evil? And who took the pages out of it? Why?"

I nodded, then turned back to the book and ran the question through my mind.

Tell me why.

The book seemed to pull at me, an unnatural tug that I'd never felt before. As my fingertips grazed the smooth leather cover, pain slammed into me, followed by a vision of the city wall. I gritted my teeth and kept contact with the book, trying to narrow in on the vision.

Where was this?

Somewhere in Guild City, definitely. I recognized the large stone blocks that made up our city wall. They had been laid in a distinctive pattern and occasionally seemed to shimmer with magic. This was definitely Guild City...but where?

I tried to memorize the stones, then opened my eyes. The interior of the book called to me, and I flipped it open, searching for the missing pages.

Dark magic seeped from the book, coating the air in a sickening, oily sheen, and I held my breath as I laid my fingertips on the stumps of the torn pages.

Who did this?

Nothing, not so much as a hint, as if there were a steel wall between me and the information.

"It's protected by a charm," I said. "Someone has used magic to conceal their actions."

"What did the pages used to say?" Seraphia asked.

I asked the question and once again hit the same wall. "I don't know. That information is hidden from me." The vision of the wall flickered in my mind. "But I'm seeing a section of the city wall. I think our answers are there. It's...pulling at me."

It felt wholly unnatural. Cursed.

I shuddered.

What the hell was going on?

2

CARROW

"Let's go find it," Mac said.

I withdrew my hand from the tome and nodded, trying to shake off the sickly feeling. "Yeah, our answers are definitely there."

"Where, exactly?" Seraphia asked.

"A section of the city wall, but where precisely...I'm not sure." I closed the leather cover, still feeling the pull from the city wall, and stood. "I think I can find it."

Seraphia jumped off the couch. "I'm coming."

I nodded at her and grabbed the book, holding it away from me. Just touching it made me feel queasy.

"Let me get a bag." I hurried to my little bedroom, which was already cluttered with clothes. The books that my dead friend Beatrix had given me had pride of place on the bedside table.

Quickly, I rifled through the old armoire that Mac had found at a car boot sale—only magic could fit an armoire into a car boot—and found the leather messenger bag inside. I stuffed the book into it, grateful to feel the magic dim.

I returned to the living room, and the three of us hurried down the stairs, spilling out onto the street. Fortunately, the rain had slowed to a faint drizzle, and the early afternoon sun was trying to peek through the clouds.

"So all you could see was a section of the city wall?" Seraphia asked.

"Yeah. I don't think I was even supposed to see that much. There's a spell on this book that's meant to stop a seer's vision, I think."

"But you're not a seer," Mac said.

"I think that's why I can see part of what the book wants to hide."

"What *are* you, exactly?" Seraphia asked.

"Um..."

She held up her hands, an apologetic look on her face. "Sorry, sorry. It's rude of me to ask."

"The truth is, I don't know what I am, exactly."

"Let's get a move on," Mac said.

I smiled at her, grateful for her ability to deftly move the conversation off me.

Seraphia nodded enthusiastically.

I turned and headed down the street, following the tug of magic that pulled me toward the edge of the city. We hurried along winding streets dotted with a variety of shops built hundreds of years earlier, their Tudor fronts—dark wooden beams, white plaster, and glittering mullioned windows—holdovers from the age of Elizabeth the First. The windows of these businesses displayed potions, weapons, spells, books, and restaurant tables set with smoking cocktails. People laughed and talked inside, magic sparking around them.

Here and there, huge trees grew out of the pavement, ancient relics of the past that had remained undisturbed for centuries. Fairy lights glittered around the branches.

The vision of the wall directed me to the gate preferred by my friends and me—one of many entrances to the city, a magical portal that led directly to the Haunted Hound pub, where Mac worked with Quinn. Before we reached the gatehouse, I was drawn to the right, and I made for an alley that was dim and dusty despite the watery sunlight.

"I don't go down here much," Mac said.

"Me neither." Seraphia stuck close to us as we entered the narrow space.

I led the way down the seemingly endless passage of brick and stone. The cobblestones beneath my feet were uneven, and the walls were without windows or doors.

"This must be the narrowest street in town," I said.

"And long." Mac moved closer to me and peered around my shoulder.

We hurried down the corridor, the walls of the buildings on either side nearly scraping against my jacket. About fifty meters later, we arrived at a clearing that separated us from the city wall.

"Ah, No Man's Square," Mac said.

"What is that?" I inspected the space. There were many clearings around town, most of them situated in front of the guild towers that punctuated the city walls at irregular intervals. In most such areas, shops and restaurants filled the buildings at the edge of the clearing, but here, the buildings were abandoned and boarded up.

"There's no guild tower in this square." Mac pointed to an empty expanse of wall that pulled at me strangely. "This area is deserted. There may have been shops and restaurants here once, but not in my lifetime."

The grass in the square was damp and scraggly, with wildflowers blooming in patches. The vegetation looked weak and limp, as though struggling to suck nutrients from the oppressive air.

The city wall, constructed of massive stones, rose tall and beckoned. "Where are we in relation to the gate that leads to the Haunted Hound?"

"Not far," Mac said. "It's to our left a few hundred meters, as the crow flies."

"Are there any guild towers between here and there?" I asked.

"No. The closest guild tower is to our right, and it's another few hundred meters away."

"So nothing really happens here." I eyed the statue of a man in the middle of the square. It was an ancient stone thing, worn and battered by time and the elements.

A bird sat on top of its head, black and regal.

"Is that Eve's raven?" I asked.

Mac tilted her head. "Maybe. But don't ask her."

Our fae friend was followed everywhere by a black raven she claimed not to see. I'd learned the hard way that she got plenty annoyed if you asked her about it.

"Who was that guy?" I asked.

"Councilor Rasla." There was a slight edge to Mac's voice. "Bloke's been dead a few hundred years, but he was the one who put the strict guild rules into place."

"That everyone must join one?" I asked. "No weirdos allowed in Guild City?"

"That's the one." Mac's lips twisted.

"Jerk."

"It explains why all the local birds are using his head for a loo." Mac pointed to the statue, which was covered in white drips.

I smiled, but even the joke wasn't enough to distract me from the tug on my soul. I slowly approached the wall, curiosity pulling at me. As I cut across the grassy square, I avoided the larger clumps of flowers that were wet from the rain. The day was too cool to get my trousers soaked.

But the closer I came to the wall, the more strongly it pulled.

It almost...*sang* to me.

I picked up the pace, forgetting my reluctance to wade through the flowers. Vaguely, I recognized that the calves of my jeans were getting wet, but I plowed onward, determined to reach the wall.

What was it about this place?

"Carrow!" Mac's voice sounded from behind me, echoing slightly with concern.

I could barely hear it.

I kept going, unable to resist the wall's siren call.

I reached it and pressed my hand to the rough, shimmering stone. *Magic.* Mac shouted my name again, but the stone wall held my attention. It pulsed, changing in temperature from cool to warm. Dark magic surrounded it, sickening me, but my fascination with the wall was stronger than my discomfort.

A vision flashed in my mind of me walking *into* the wall, stepping through the stone, which should be impossible.

What happened here?

I asked the question but got no answer. Again, that steel barrier flew up between the information and my vision. This place was also protected by a spell.

But something happened here.

I pressed my hand harder to the stone, desperate to figure it out.

"Carrow!" Mac's voice was at my ear now, and her hands wrapped around my arms. She pulled me back, yanking hard.

My hand broke contact with the wall, and I stumbled against Mac. Her arms tightened around me.

"What's going on?" I asked, struggling in her grasp.

"You went into some kind of trance."

I turned and caught sight of her white face. Seraphia stood next to her, a frown drawing her eyebrows together. "It was strange, Carrow," said the librarian. "As you neared the building, you seemed to...disappear, almost."

"And your eyes are glowing again," Mac said.

Shit. I looked back at the wall. It still pulsed with magic. "I don't understand. It calls to me, but it's so dark."

"Because of Orion's Heart?" Mac asked.

"I don't know."

I looked back at her and frowned. A dark light seemed to surround her. It came from the wall, creeping along the ground and up her legs. Seraphia glowed, too. They were standing close enough that the magic reached them.

"Mac..." I touched her shoulder gently, but she didn't feel any different. "You're pale."

"I—" Her brow creased, and she grimaced, folding over on herself. "I don't feel well," she gasped.

"Me, either," Seraphia said, going to her knees.

Panic flared. "What's happened?"

"A curse." Mac straightened, her entire body shaking. "It's the wall, somehow. I can feel it."

I looked back. The wall glowed with dark magic, magic that had infected Mac and Seraphia. My heart raced. "How do we fix you?"

"Let's go to Eve." Mac looked at me, confusion flickering in her eyes. "Do you not feel bad?"

"Not really, no." I swallowed hard. Why was I so different?

It wasn't that I wanted to be cursed, but...

why not me, too?

"You have the faint darkness to you, though." Seraphia staggered upright. "The curse seems to be hovering around you."

Maybe it likes me.

It was a terrible thought.

"We need to get you to Eve," I said.

"We also need to figure out what the hell this is." Mac pointed to the wall, her voice firmer. "She can't fix us if we don't know what the curse is."

"Have you ever heard of anyone being cursed by a wall?" Even the words sounded insane.

"No." Mac shook her head. "But objects can hold curses, and this is a particularly big object."

"Then how did it get cursed? And with what?" I clenched my fist, resisting the urge to touch it. It was hard, though. The darkness in the stones called to me.

But I don't want to be that person.

I turned from the wall.

"We can get ourselves to Eve," Mac said. "But we need you to figure out what's going on. Are you okay here alone?"

"Yeah. Fine." I stepped away from the wall, hoping to fight its fascination. The weight of my bag pulled at my shoulder, the book reminding me of its presence. "Seraphia, have you found anything else about this in the library?"

"Nothing. I checked the entire history section, too, hoping to find a clue about the missing pages."

I nodded. "Okay. I know someone to ask."

Mac's gaze flicked to mine. "The Devil?"

Seraphia's eyes widened. "The Devil of Darkvale?"

I nodded. "He's immortal and helped found Guild City. He's the only one I know who was around when any of this happened. Surely he has to know what is going on here."

Seraphia nodded, but her tone was clipped with wariness. "If you say so."

"Come on, pal." Mac reached a supporting arm around Seraphia. "You're looking pretty pale. We need to get you to Eve."

"Thanks." Seraphia shot Mac a grateful look, as if she were unused to such kindness.

"Update me as soon as Eve helps you," I said.

"Likewise," Mac said. "I want to know what the hell is going on here."

I nodded, watching them turn and limp across the grassy square. At one point, they fell to their knees, and fear surged through me, blocking my throat.

This could kill them.

The wall still pulled at me. Everything in my soul wanted me to turn around and press my entire body against it.

Nope.

The sight of Mac and Seraphia dragging themselves to their feet gave me the strength to resist. I kept my gaze on the two women for support as I followed them away from the overgrown square. Exiting the dingy alley, I made for the Devil's tower. Grey's tower, as I now thought of it.

It had been three days since I'd appeared before the council with Grey at my side. Three days since I'd seen him, but I had a problem, a big problem that I didn't fully understand.

And I was going to bring that problem straight to the devil himself.

3

CARROW

The journey to Grey's tower was a blur. People thronged the streets, shopping or out for lunch, but the wall and the curse surrounding it were the only things on my mind.

We'd *just* saved Guild City from a deadly threat. Was I now going to have to save my friends from another one?

I wasn't sure I was up for the job.

But I had to be.

Finally, I reached the clearing in front of Grey's tall, dark tower. Powerful and mysterious, Grey had been here since the city was founded. He owned his own tower, the only individual who could make that claim.

The black stone was imposing, and the red glass in the windows emphasized that this was the Devil's lair.

The truth of him was far more complicated, I'd come to learn.

The two bouncers at the door nodded in recognition. Both were shifters, members of the guild that handled security and protection details in town. One was a lion and the other a panther, if I recalled correctly. I returned the gesture, hurrying past them and into the small foyer of the Devil's domain.

As usual, Miranda stood at the desk. She was dressed impeccably in her uniform of pencil skirt, blouse, and stilettos, her hair pulled back in a neat twist at the base of her neck.

Only the uninitiated would think that the beautiful banshee was just a hostess.

"You're here to see him?" asked Grey's right-hand woman.

"I am."

She raised her comms charm to her lips and spoke into it, murmuring low. I could hear the faint echo of Grey's voice as he answered her, but it was too quiet for me to make out.

She lowered the device and looked up at me. "I'll take you."

"Thanks."

She gestured for me to follow her and strode down the hall, her tall heels clicking against the floor.

Somehow, I just knew she was the kind of woman who could run in those things. She could probably even blind a man with them, all without so much as slipping them off.

We passed by Grey's nightclub. It was almost certainly a front for his illegal business dealings, but I was confident he didn't do anything too ethically questionable. The Council held such tight control over Guild City's magic that smuggling allowed Grey to make a fortune without dealing in people, weapons, or drugs, like so many human mobsters did.

Miranda passed Grey's office and kept going toward his private quarters.

My brows rose. It was well into the workday already, but he was seeing me in his living space?

As always, I wanted to ask Miranda more about Grey. There was so much that I didn't know about my Cursed Mate.

But I'd be a fool to ask.

She'd never betray him, not with so much as a morsel of information.

She stopped outside of Grey's chambers and rapped on the door.

A moment later, it swung open. Grey's tall form filled the doorway, and he was so handsome that he nearly burned my eyes. As usual, he wore one of his impeccable suits. He looked like a spy right out of a James Bond film in the elegant apparel. His sharp cheekbones and strong jaw were highlighted by a faint stream of light coming from the window, but it was his full lips that drew and held my gaze.

"Thank you, Miranda." His low voice feathered over my nerve endings.

Miranda nodded and disappeared silently. I met his icy gray gaze. It warmed slightly at the sight of me.

"Grey."

"Carrow." He gestured for me to enter. "To what do I owe this pleasure?"

"I'm not sure it's going to be a pleasure."

"Any time spent with you is, regardless of the circumstances."

"Um..." I didn't know what to say in response to his smoothness.

I stepped into the main living room, struck again by how pristine and perfect it was. It was austere, yes, but so was he. At least on the outside. Like him, the space was gorgeous. An enormous glass window provided a view of a moonlit beach. Massive waves crashed on a rocky shore, the pale light making them sparkle like diamonds. It was magic, but it looked real. Through the bedroom door, I could see a sliver of the grand piano that sat in the corner.

The lid was up, as if he'd recently been playing.

It hadn't been up last time. Then, the piano had looked untouched for years. Centuries, maybe. The thin layer of dust on it and the air of neglect had been hard to miss.

"Have you been playing the piano?" I hoped so. If he *had* been, I liked to think it was because of me, an indicator that he cared about me.

Crazy and fanciful, maybe, but hell, *I* was crazy and fanciful.

He nodded. "Yes."

I raised my brows, hoping he would continue. Of course, he didn't.

We weren't there in our relationship. I cared for him more than I wanted to admit—more than made sense, even—but now wasn't the time. I had Mac and Seraphia to think about.

"Can I offer you anything?" Grey leaned against a heavy armchair, relaxed and casual, a predator, a lion lounging on the Savannah, ready to strike.

Oddly, I wanted him to. I shivered.

"No, thank you." *We're Cursed Mates!* I wanted to scream. But we still didn't even know what that meant.

"Are you here about the Council and joining a guild?"

"No."

Though I should be more worried about that, considering my status. I didn't belong to a guild. None would have me, as we'd both recently learned. A few days ago at a ceremony to help me find my place in Guild City, I'd been rejected by all.

It didn't matter that I didn't particularly want to join one. I'd wanted the option, for God's sake. I needed to be a member of a guild to stay in the city. As things stood, my days here were numbered. Especially since some Council members seemed to hate my guts, like Ubhan the sorcerer. Miserable bastard.

I shook the thought away.

"I thought I'd see you before now." I nearly slapped a hand to my mouth. I hadn't meant to admit that. It was like saying I cared for him.

I *did* care for him, but I'd never tell him. Once we'd learned we were Cursed Mates, we'd agreed not to pursue the attraction between us. It was too dangerous.

Even so, he'd asked me to stay with him after the Council meeting three days earlier. I'd said no. I was afraid, afraid of how quickly things were moving between us and of our status as Cursed Mates. He, it seemed, had temporarily lost his mind when he'd asked me, and now I'd lost mine by admitting that I'd hoped to see him.

Cool and collected, nerd. Play it cool and collected.

"It's too dangerous," he said.

"Of course. Because of the Cursed Mates thing."

He nodded. "You had a vision of me drinking you to the death. I can't ignore that."

I shivered at the memory. Obviously, he was right. We didn't know the exact specifics of our situation, but we knew enough.

"I'm trying to figure out why we are what we are," Grey said. "And how we can stop it. Until then, I thought it wise to avoid it entirely."

"Avoid me, you mean." I nodded, trying to appear nonchalant. "Clever."

The briefest pain flickered in his eyes, and I wondered about the piano. Did he play that when he was distraught?

Did a man like him even *become* distraught?

That was probably the wrong word for it.

"Fate has plans for us," he said. "Being Cursed Mates is rare—exceedingly so. Until we know exactly what lies in store for us and how to avoid it, it's too dangerous. But when I learn more, you'll be the first to know."

Until then, it was just...*this*. Distance.

It made sense. There was no arguing with something so rational.

I shoved away thoughts of pianos and Cursed Mates and handsome vampires. I had far bigger problems right now, and the Cursed Mates thing could be dealt with later. Especially if we kept trying to ignore what was between us.

I pulled the book from my bag and held it out to him. "This is why I'm here."

He frowned at it, then met my gaze. "What is the issue, specifically?"

I flipped open the book and showed him the missing pages. "Someone tore them out, then enchanted the book so that I couldn't see who did it or what the pages were about."

"I have a feeling this is about more than a vandalized book."

"A lot more." I could tell him all about it, but it'd be far better to show him. "I need you to come with me."

The Devil

Carrow led me through the bustling streets of Guild City, her stride long and confident. I couldn't keep my gaze off her golden hair. It glinted in the weak sunlight. She'd given me back the full range of my vision. Thanks to her, I could see color again, taste things as they were meant to be, *feel* things.

She had brought me back to life.

I reached out for her, an unconscious gesture that shocked the hell out of me. Quickly, I curled my hand into a fist, lowering it to my side.

Cursed Mate.

I hadn't lied when I'd said that I was trying to learn the specifics of the phenomenon, but it was proving to be exceedingly difficult.

Her vision and the title of our affliction itself were

clear enough. We were fated to be together, yet cursed to be torn apart. By me drinking her to the death.

How the hell that would happen, though, I had no idea.

There was something in me...this driving *force*...that compelled me to protect her. I hadn't felt something so strong since the blood lust when I'd first been turned. But this...

I couldn't let anything bad happen to her.

And this was all my fault. My touch was tainted. It had been so since I was turned. How could I be anything other than her Cursed Mate?

The obvious solution was to ignore her and us, but Carrow was hard to forget. It had been impossible *not* to think of her, and I was accustomed to avoiding things.

Things that I wanted.

I'd never wanted a person before—not like this— and it took everything I had to fight the pull between us. No matter how much I wanted her, the *Cursed* part of our situation hung over our heads.

"Where, exactly, are we going?" I asked, trying to drag my attention from her.

"Almost there."

She led me down a narrow alley between build-ings. The rough stone snagged the fabric of my suit, and I shifted so that I could move silently through the space.

We arrived in a quiet square at the edge of town. It

was familiar—every place in Guild City was familiar—but I hadn't been there in decades. Centuries, possibly.

"What's happening here?" I frowned at the wall, feeling the faintest pulse of dark magic. I stepped toward it, and Carrow grabbed my arm. Awareness raced through me at her touch, and I suppressed the faintest shudder.

"Don't go near it," she warned. "There's dark magic around the wall. It cursed Mac and Seraphia."

"Seraphia? The librarian?"

"Yes. You know her?"

"Not well. But I quite like the library." I hadn't read much in decades, but the library was quiet and imbued with an energy that soothed me when the memories became too dark. It was a meditative place for me.

I turned to look at her and stilled. "What's wrong with your eyes?"

She snapped them shut. "Are they glowing?"

"Yes." She stepped away from the wall and opened them again. The bright green faded to its normal hue. "I don't know why they do that. Maybe something to do with Orion's Heart?"

"The magic you absorbed."

"Exactly. But let's deal with this right now."

"Which is what, pray tell?"

"It has to do with this history book." She pulled it out of her bag once more, opening it to the missing pages. "It's imbued with an evil magic that matches the curse on this wall. And the pages that have been torn out talk about the history of Guild City...or so we assume. We don't know what they said."

Understanding dawned. "And I'm the only one old enough to know what would have happened back then. I'm your first-hand account."

"Exactly." Worry creased her brow. "Which makes you my only hope for Mac and Seraphia. They've been cursed by this, but I have no idea how or by what."

"You weren't cursed?" Worry tugged.

She shook her head, her lips pinched. "No. And I don't know why."

"Good."

She nodded, her pleading gaze meeting mine. "Tell me why this place is cursed. How do I fix Mac and Seraphia?"

I turned to the wall, searching my memory. It came up blank, which wasn't surprising, given the length of my life and all the things I'd forgot over the years, but I hated that I couldn't immediately fix her problem. "I genuinely don't know."

"You don't remember any of the important things that happened here? Hangings or festivals or crimes?"

"You think a past event might have stained this place?"

"Maybe." She shrugged. "I'm reaching, here. I want to know how this wall could curse Mac and Seraphia, and I know the past has something to do with it."

"I'm sorry, I don't remember anything interesting about this place." In normal life, I wasn't above lying about what I knew. But with Carrow, I was compelled to speak the truth.

And regretfully, I had.

"What?" Surprise flickered in her voice. "How can you not remember?"

"Do you remember everything from your entire life?"

"Well...no. But this is important."

"Many important things have happened in the last five hundred years." I winced. "Closer to six hundred, now."

Resignation flickered on her face, and maybe something like concern.

For me?

No. Of course not.

People thought immortality was a gift. And maybe it would be, if everyone lived forever, but they didn't.

Therefore, it was a lonely proposition.

"What do you know about that man?" She pointed to the statue.

"Councilor Rasla was a bastard, but I don't remember him well." I frowned, trying to recall details about him. Rasla had been pivotal in establishing the rule of law in Guild City. Why were my memories of him vague?

I rubbed the bridge of my nose, fighting a headache.

A *headache*?

Since when did I get headaches?

"Are you all right?" Carrow asked.

"Yes. Fine." I met her gaze. "You want to know what I know about this place?"

"Yes." Frustration vibrated from her.

"Well, then. We'll reach into my memory."

4

I frowned at Grey, my frustration turning to confusion. "Reach into your memory?"

"Just because I can't immediately recall everything that happened to me doesn't mean I can't access it. Finding a way to remember events in my past has been vital to building my empire."

"So, you have a lot of journals or something?"

A low chuckle burst from him. "Not precisely."

"Good, because I really don't want to sort through hundreds of years of your handwritten journals." *Lie.* Even though the idea of him sitting down and penning his life story was ridiculous—he was *so* not that kind of man—I did want the insight. Desperately.

"It's not quite my style," he said.

"No. I imagine not."

"I have a Mind Mage who helps me recover my stored memories. We'll go to her and find the information that you seek. Unless you want to try?"

"I'm not sure my gift works for that, but I could try."

He held out his arm, and I rested my fingertips on his sleeve, the warmth of his skin sending a shiver through me.

"Remember that I can't vow that I ever knew the information you seek," he said.

I nodded and called upon my magic, trying to see whatever might be lost inside his head.

Nothing happened.

I tried again.

Still nothing. I removed my hand and met his gaze. "I think we need to go see your Mind Mage."

He nodded. "Come, then. We'll visit the Mages' Guild tower."

I grinned, the faintest bit of excitement pushing through my worry. I'd never been to the mages' tower. I'd visited the guild towers belonging to the witches, the sorcerers, and the dwarves, but none of the others. "Lead on."

He nodded and turned, striding back down the narrow alley. I followed, admiring the way he moved smoothly through the narrow space, twisted slightly to avoid brushing the stone walls with his broad shoulders. He walked on silent feet, the ultimate predator.

We reached the main street a few minutes later, and it was still bustling with people hauling shopping bags and chatting away in groups.

"Where do the mages live?" I asked, wondering if we could swing by Eve's shop to check on Mac and Seraphia.

"Far side of town, near the witches."

I did the map in my head—one of my gifts—and frowned. No way we could quickly stop by to check on them, not without a long delay. I sent Eve a text instead, hoping for a reply.

I followed Grey down the street, sticking close to his side on the narrow sidewalk. Passersby parted like the Red Sea for Moses, and we made rapid progress. Soon, we neared one of the larger intersections in town. Though there were no cars in Guild City, it buzzed with motorbike traffic.

A tiny figure caught my eye, and I stopped.

Cordelia darted across the road, her tiny paws swiftly carrying her fluffy body. The raccoon darted around the bikes, narrowly avoiding collision. Shouts and horns announced the drivers' irritation. She grinned back at them, a gleeful little bandit with fangs.

"Your familiar is a hazard." There was a hint of affection to Grey's voice, and I recalled that he could understand Cordelia, the only person other than me who could. That had to mean something, right?

"I don't see any collisions." I grinned as the raccoon stopped on the sidewalk in front of me, standing up on her hind legs. "What's up, Cordelia?"

Eve wants that book.

I looked down at the sack that hung heavily from my shoulder. It seemed to weigh far more than a book should, and I'd be grateful to get rid of it. "Do you think you can carry it?"

She scoffed.

I looked at Grey. "If the mages need it for any reason, Cordelia can bring it back to us."

"I doubt they will. My contact has the skill to read my memories, but not that book."

I unlooped the bag from around my neck and passed it down to Cordelia. "How are they doing?"

So-so. Worry glinted in her little black eyes. *But this might help, Eve said.*

"Be careful with it."

She scoffed again, as if delivering cursed books was her usual afternoon—which it very well might be—then tightened the bag strap with her little hands, tying a knot in it so that it was incredibly short. She swung it across her body, balancing it on her broad little back, then turned tail and darted across the street. A chorus of shouts and horns followed her, but she ignored them.

"I didn't think raccoons could do that," Grey said.

"She's not just any raccoon."

"Fair enough." He started across the narrow street, striding quickly. I followed, and soon, we neared the edge of town.

As usual, there was an open square between the town and the guild tower that adjoined the castle walls. I stared at the Mages' Guild tower in awe. It was one of the most fantastic examples of Tudor architecture I'd ever seen. Unlike most of the period buildings, this one was enormous. Four stories tall, it was constructed entirely of dark beams and white plaster, like something out of Shakespeare.

Mullioned glass windows gleamed in the sun, and the sharply slanted roof was tiled in the dark stone. In classic Tudor fashion, the upper floors protruded farther out than those below. The structure seemed slightly uneven, as though the ground had shifted over the last five hundred years and the building had followed suit, making it slant to the left.

The square in front of the tower was a beautifully manicured garden filled with carefully trimmed hedges, roses, and pebbled paths.

"It's the finest example of an Elizabethan garden in the world," Grey said.

"And human historians have no idea it exists."

"Not a clue." He led me through the garden, past delicate benches and little ponds, until we reached the entrance to the tower. He reached for the door.

"We're just going to walk in?" I thought of the carefully guarded Sorcerers' Guild tower. "They won't get angry?"

"We're going into the public space." He pulled on the door, and noise rushed out—talking and laughing and the sound of a kettle screeching.

I gasped at the sight inside.

It was a coffee shop—the most fabulous coffee shop I'd ever seen. Grey held the door open for me, and I stepped into the low-ceilinged room. Tiny tables were clustered around the space, but my eyes were drawn to the bar manned by several swift-looking individuals with wild haircuts and pierced ears. It was a look shared by baristas in the trendy cafés and tearooms of London, with one difference. Here, the espresso machines resembled something out of a steampunk fantasist's dreams, with coiled copper tubing, whirling dials, and colorful steam all operating at top speed.

A shining gold sign glittered over the bar—*The Mages' Coffeehouse.*

Hallways and stairs leading off the main room provided glimpses of the other areas of the coffee house. It appeared huge, with booths and cozy nooks to suit the most exacting coffee enthusiast.

To my right was a sleek, modern room with a separate entrance filled with harried businesspeople buzzing in for a quick bite or takeaway coffee.

"It looks just like central London," I mused.

"We have our fair share of office drones in Guild City," Grey said, "though they tend to be sequestered behind ancient glass and creaky beams. Not like the high-rises of London."

He didn't sound bitter about the changes in London, as I might have imagined another ancient supernatural would be. People tended to cling to their past and the way things were, but not Grey. Instead, he sounded impressed.

In the room next to the takeaway café, a jazz band played for the enjoyment of patrons drinking tiny cups of espresso. On the other side of the main room, students bent over tables, their noses stuck in books as they drank tall, frothy glasses of iced beverages. Another room was full of books and records. There, I spotted three witches I'd met when I'd first arrived in town.

Mary, Beth, and Coraline were all dressed in brightly colored, mismatched outfits, and they laughed over something in the book in front of them. Beth spotted me and waved. I waved back, then turned to Grey. "Why do the mages have a coffee shop? It's not what I might have expected from magic users who can control the elements."

"I'm not entirely sure why they've kept it up, but the guild opened the first coffeehouse in the seventeenth century, when they became popular in London. The leader of the guild at that time was enamored with them and wanted to have one here."

"He seems to have nailed it."

"Yes. He did."

"Who are we meeting, then?"

"A Mind Mage named Genara. She's a bit unusual for a mage. They tend to control the elements, as you noted, but she's one of the rare ones who can read minds."

"Read minds?" *Yikes.*

He nodded. "Come. We'll head up to the room she prefers."

"There's *more*?"

"A lot more." He led the way toward one of the rickety, dark wooden staircases at the back.

I eyed the espresso machines whirling away behind the bar, vowing to return for a drink, then followed him up the creaking stairs.

We passed a room that appeared to be an ice cream parlor. The barista poured a shot of espresso over a scoop of ice cream, then topped it with a dash of liqueur from a sparkling crystal glass.

Yes, I would be returning. Definitely.

Grey led me to a room on the third level. The floor sloped downward toward the street, the ancient wooden beams shifting silently underfoot. The walls and ceiling were as dark as the floor, and I had a hunch my flat would look like this if it had never been modernized.

Tiny tables filled the room, half of them full of chatting patrons. The place was dead silent, however, and the air sparkled around each table.

"This is the privacy room," Grey said. "Each table is protected by a charm that ensures silence."

My mind went immediately to my police training. "They could be doing all kinds of illegal dealings."

"Yep."

"Have you had meetings here?"

"No need. I can have them in my office."

Of course. I eyed a woman sitting by the fire. Her dark hair was threaded with silver, and her face was lightly lined. She could have been anywhere from fifty to a hundred and fifty, and she was *beautiful*. She watched us with bright green eyes as we approached. She had to be Genara.

Grey stopped in front of her table, and she flicked her hand. Magic sparked against my skin, and suddenly, I could hear again. No voices, since no one was audibly talking, but the faint rustling of fabric and the creak of the wooden floor that I'd been missing earlier returned.

"Devil." Genara shifted, her black dress rustling slightly. "It has been a while."

"Indeed." He gestured to the chairs. "May we sit?"

"But of course." Her gaze flicked to me, and I immediately remembered what Grey had said about her ability to read minds.

Could she read my mind right now?

"Yes." Genara smiled directly at me.

Oh, crap. Don't think anything stupid. Or embarrassing.

"Don't worry," she said. "I don't share what I see. If I did, I would quickly become unpopular."

"Thanks." I stole a quick glance at Grey, wondering if she could read his thoughts so easily.

We sat in the two small chairs across from her, and she gestured to the center of the round table. "Please order whatever you like."

I eyed the empty table, confused. A moment later, magic shimmered. Golden light swirled over the wood, and images of various coffees appeared, floating in midair. There was a tiny espresso, a larger flat white, a foamy cappuccino, a mug of tea, and a few others I didn't recognize.

Grey pointed to the espresso, and I wasn't surprised by his choice. Dark and intense, just like him. The cup floated to the table, transitioning from transparent to solid as it went. The rich scent filled the air, and I considered my options, deciding upon the cappuccino.

It floated toward me, and I took it. "Thank you." The first sip was divine, and I sighed. "This is the best thing I've ever had."

"Of course it is. We only serve the best here." Genara nodded, then looked at Grey. "You are here to remember."

"Yes."

"What is it that you seek?"

5

GREY

What did I seek?

The Mind Mage's words echoed in my mind, more probing than she'd probably meant them to be.

My gaze flicked to Carrow, and I had my answer

Her.

But right now, we needed information about a past I couldn't remember. In truth, there was much that I couldn't remember. So much in my long and terrible past that had been replaced by new memories.

The terrible things remained, of course. Humans had that uncanny ability to recall their worst times, and I was no exception. The best times?

Those were so few and far between. And now that

I'd met Carrow, they all paled in comparison to what I felt for her.

No.

I knew what was in our future—she'd seen it herself. I would drink her to death, according to her vision. Though we might not know exactly why, that was enough information for me.

I couldn't have her.

I could never have her.

It would be easy enough to say that I'd never do the terrible deed, but I'd seen enough to respect magic and fate. The only way to be sure I could control myself was to avoid her as much as possible.

I blinked and turned toward Genara. She could read minds from a distance, but not mine, thank fates. My inner self was locked tight. It had taken years of practice to achieve that protection, but I considered it time well spent.

She could see into my mind if I permitted, and only if she were touching me. Even then, she couldn't see all the way. Rather, her skills helped me unlock memories that were long forgotten.

"There is a place in Guild City with a past that I might know more about." I explained everything that Carrow had told me and that I had seen, including information about the book. "I believe I know some-thing about it, but that information is beyond my reach."

Genara nodded, all business now. "Of course. I can help you access it."

I leaned toward her slightly, and she raised a pale, slender hand. Golden bangles clanked at her wrist, the gems sparkling under the glow of the lamps. Her eyes met mine. "May I?"

"Yes."

As her hand moved toward my temple, I looked at Carrow. She watched, interested. She seemed to have forgotten her coffee.

Genara's cool fingertips touched my temple, and I forced back a shudder of distaste. Carrow's touch I enjoyed...but only hers. Everyone else's was a burden, even Genara's.

"Focus on what you want to know," she murmured.

I felt her magic flow from her fingers into my mind, sparking through my head as her power attempted to unlock my memories. It took all my will not to fling her away. The beast inside me did not appreciate the riskiness of this endeavor. Connection with anyone—particularly connection through the mind—was dangerous.

But I was more powerful than the beast. These days, at least. I forced it to quiet, letting Genara's magic flow through me as I tried to recall the past that was locked up tight.

Nothing came.

I frowned and tried harder, thinking of everything that Carrow had told me and everything I'd seen. That should have acted as a road map pointing me toward the part of my mind that I'd forgotten. With Genara's help, I should have been able to unlock it.

But I couldn't.

Why not?

Carrow set her coffee cup down, her hands twitching as if she wanted to try again now that there was someone who could teach her. The interest in her eyes glowed more keenly.

"Would you like to try?" I asked. "Perhaps Genara can show you."

Genara's eyes widened. "And give a possible competitor the drop on me?"

"I would never," Carrow said. "I'm just interested in learning."

Genara scoffed. "Hmm."

"Your power is not working yet," I said. "I can feel it inside me, but I remember nothing. Perhaps your gift and Carrow's combined can find what is lost."

"Fine." Genara held out her hand for Carrow. "Take my hand."

Carrow gripped her hand gently, her gaze fixed on me.

"Now touch the Devil's other temple with the fingertips of your free hand."

Carrow's fingers rested gently against the skin of my temple. Heat and comfort surged through me, tempting me to lean into her touch.

I stiffened, unwilling to show any interest or weakness. Their fingertips still rested against my head, and I forced myself to stay still. I hated this, but it was often worth it.

Genara gave Carrow directions, explaining how her magic worked and how Carrow could mimic it. Carrow's power flowed through me, feeling like pleasure and pain all at once. I should hate it like I hated Genara's touch, but I didn't.

I thought of the past, of trying to dredge up the lost memories. The harder I tried, the farther they seemed to recede behind a barrier between me and what I sought.

Carrow gasped and jerked her hand back, her eyes wide. "Something is wrong."

Irritation and confusion pricked at me. She was right.

I looked at Genara. "What's going on?"

"I think there's a block on your memory." She frowned. "I've never seen anything quite like that before."

"What do you mean, a block? I've forgotten something forever?"

"No, not quite. More like a curse, cast by another."

"I've been cursed?" My heartbeat thundered, and I stilled, senses on high alert. My predator senses were unlike my normal human senses, which had been dulled when I'd first been turned. These were something almost unnatural, allowing me to find prey and fellow predators alike.

"Perhaps." She shrugged. "I don't know what is happening inside your mind, but I suspect someone doesn't want you to remember something. That is all I know."

My jaw tightened, and I stood. "Thank you for your assistance."

Carrow stood as well, shooting a confused glance between Genara and me. I reached into my pocket, withdrew a golden coin, and laid it on the table. Like many mages, Genara preferred to be paid in the old manner, and I kept a coin on me for such cases.

I turned, Carrow followed, and we wound our way between the tables and down the stairs. We passed through the main part of the coffee shop, and the witches in the book room smiled when they spotted her. They rose, hesitated as their gazes met mine, then sat back down.

Carrow hurried up next to me. "This is very bad, isn't it?"

"It's bad." I stepped out onto the city street and drew in a fresh breath of air, working to calm my mind. The quiet of the garden beckoned, and I strode toward it, finding a spot in the middle that was far from any buildings or prying ears, before I turned to Carrow. "I've never been unable to access my memories before."

She frowned up at me. "Whoever tore those pages

out of the book didn't want anyone to know what they did."

"And I was the only person who would outlive them, so they had to erase whatever I knew." Anger tightened my muscles. Having my mind manipulated was an invasion. It made me want to crush something. I clenched my fists, determined to remain outwardly calm. "Who the hell has fucked with my memory? Can you get that information with your gift? Not what Genara taught you, but *your* gift."

"By touching you?" She frowned. "I can try, but my gift doesn't work well on you. The only thing I've ever seen is information about us being Cursed Mates."

"Try. Please."

She nodded, raising a hand to grip my wrist. Her touch sent heat shooting through me, and I grounded myself with the feeling. Immediately, it calmed some of my helpless rage.

"You feel different," she said.

"What do you mean?"

"Not as angry."

"I *felt* angry?"

She nodded. "Like, your aura. I couldn't see it on you. You never show emotion like that. Cold as ice, like normal. But you had this...energy."

"I'm fine now. Don't worry."

She scoffed. "Hell, I'd be angry, too, if someone messed with my mind."

"I'll find them."

She nodded and closed her eyes. Her magic flowed through me, lighting me up like a bonfire. I shifted, trying to fight the pull that dragged me toward her. Drawing in a slow breath, I focused on my self-control.

Eventually, she opened her eyes and withdrew her hand. "I can't get anything." She scowled. "If I could go touch the wall again, maybe I could get more information from it."

"No." I shook my head. "It's too dangerous. Whoever we're dealing with was powerful enough to manipulate my mind. I don't want you going up against them."

"They might be dead. There's no telling when this happened. Could be hundreds of years ago."

"Could be. It's still too dangerous."

"I'm afraid that's not your call to make."

I resisted the growl that had no place in civilized conversation. "More's the pity. We need to try to find another copy of the book. See what this bastard is hiding."

"Seraphia said there aren't any more copies in her library."

"There could be another copy somewhere else. And if there is, I know someone who would know. Nevaeh Cross, a researcher at the X in Magic Side, Chicago."

"Is that another magical town?"

"It's Chicago's version of Guild City, or the Grassmarket neighborhood in Edinburgh. Hidden from human eyes but visible to supernaturals."

"Let's go to her."

"I'll contact her and tell her what we're looking for. It could take her a bit of time to find what we seek."

She opened her mouth to argue, but her mobile buzzed. She pulled it from her pocket and silently read the text before meeting my gaze. "Looks like Eve is making some progress with Mac and Seraphia. They're stable."

"Go check on them." The sun glowed orange behind her as it sank toward the horizon. "It's nearly night. Get some rest. I'll let you know when Ms. Cross has a lead."

She nodded. "Be careful."

The hint of concern in her voice warmed me, though I knew such weakness on my part was dangerous. "I will. I'll update you no later than tomorrow morning."

She nodded, then turned and left. I stared hungrily after her. Foolish, perhaps, but I couldn't help myself.

6

CARROW

My mind spun with all that I'd learned as I headed through the winding passages of Guild City. Old cast-iron streetlamps flickered to life, throwing a golden glow on the shop windows that jostled with magic and life.

Bars were filling up—happy hour was a thing, even in the magical world—and cheerful supernaturals passed me in groups as they headed toward their usual haunts.

This was all still new to me. Normally, I'd spend time exploring as I walked, peering in shop windows and daydreaming about my life in Guild City, but my thoughts were on Mac and Seraphia.

I reached Eve's place in record time, panting, my

skin lightly dampened with sweat. I pushed open the door and stepped inside. The main shop was empty, but Eve's voice echoed from the back room. "Who is it?"

"Carrow."

"Come on back."

I hurried through the shop, passing shelves of tiny vials and jars of potion. Eve relegated her dangerous potions to the back room, where she did a lot of her work.

It was chaos.

Every surface was covered with the tools of her trade: small cauldrons, knives, a mortar and pestle, along with jars and bowls of ingredients. The fae's hair was bright pink. A few days ago, it had been purple and white. The raven that followed her everywhere sat high on a shelf, observing the situation below.

Mac and Seraphia stood nearby. They looked better than when I'd last seen them. Their color was back, and their eyes were brighter.

"How are you feeling?" I hurried toward them, carefully inspecting their faces for any signs of distress.

"Fine now." Mac grinned to reassure me, and Seraphia mimicked her smile.

Worry and guilt streaked through me. Why were they cursed if I wasn't?

"I don't buy it." I turned to Eve. "How are they?"

"Fine for the moment." Concern flickered in her eyes. "I got a few clues from the cursed book, enough to make a potion to hold off the effects, but I wasn't able to cure them."

"Not yet," Mac said. "You'll figure it out."

"Grey is looking for another copy," I told them. "Maybe if we figure out what history was erased, we'll learn more about the curse."

Eve's brows rose. "*Grey*, is it?"

I shrugged. I hadn't yet confessed that I'd started calling him by his first name, but Eve didn't stick on the question.

"But that's good," she said. "If we can find out who cast the curse, then it'll be easier to cure. Different supernaturals have different abilities, and it will narrow down our search if we know what the culprit was capable of."

"We're going to be fine," Mac said. "You're the best there is."

"But I haven't found an antidote yet," Eve said. "Hell, we don't even know what's going to happen to you."

"But you whipped up something to hold off the effects, so we're good." Mac squeezed her hand. "We've got this, don't worry."

I looked between Mac and Eve, worry streaking through me. Mac was putting on a brave face, but this was bad.

Seraphia met my gaze. "How did it go with the Devil? What did you learn besides the fact that he'll seek another copy of *A Most Elucidating History of Guild City*?"

I explained about his memory and our hopes to unlock it.

"I like that plan," Mac said.

"He said he'll meet you tomorrow morning?" Seraphia asked.

"Yes. His friend will hopefully have a copy of the book by then."

"Good," Eve said, "because these two need to rest. I don't want them getting too tired or weak. It could give the curse a better foothold on them."

I nodded. "Let's head up to my place. We'll get some food, rest, and come up with a game plan. There's probably something we're missing."

Mac grinned. "Like a girls' night!"

"A girls' night with a goal," I said. "And an early bedtime."

"Of course. But I like this plan." She looked at Seraphia. "Will you come?"

"Me?"

"Yeah, you, silly. We need to go over all the facts again. But more importantly, you're cool, and you should come hang out with us."

Seraphia smiled. "Okay."

"Let's do my flat," I suggested.

"I'm going to leave everything like it is and lock up," Eve said. "I can clean this mess tomorrow."

"Good plan," I said, and shepherded the others toward the front.

It took her less than half a minute to finish her stuff and grab her keys. I got the history book, and we headed out of her shop, Eve and Seraphia in the lead.

I hung back with Mac. "Are you really okay?"

"Yeah." She nudged me with her shoulder. "Don't worry so much."

"And Seraphia?"

"She's fine, too."

"She seems a bit lonely." I thought back to her eyes. "Not sure why. Just something about her."

"She keeps to herself, mostly. In our world, you tend not to poke when someone does that. You never know what they're hiding."

"But you trust her?"

"Yeah. I think she's got a bad past, but I trust her. And no one should be lonely."

"You like to collect strays."

"Strays?"

"Yeah." I grinned and pointed to myself. "Like me. Now Seraphia."

Mac shrugged. "What can I say? There aren't really any stray cats in town, and you're the next best thing."

I laughed, and the four of us headed up to my place, taking the stairs two at a time.

When we passed Mac's door, she paused. "Do you have wine?"

I scoffed. "Do I have wine? Only the finest adult juice boxes in all the land."

Mac laughed. "Those little single-serving boxes?"

"The very same. If you're lucky, I'll give you a straw."

Her brows rose, interest gleaming in her eyes. "Fantastic. I'll get some crisps."

"If Cordelia hasn't eaten them all."

"Fingers crossed." She darted into her place.

"Thanks."

Eve and Seraphia reached my door first. "Let yourself in," I said, gesturing. "It's unlocked."

"You should lock it," Seraphia said. "This place isn't as safe as it seems."

I frowned at her. She wasn't wrong, but the way she said it...

She shifted and looked away, then followed Eve into the flat.

Yeah, Seraphia had a tricky past, all right. But it was none of my business unless she wanted to share, so I put it aside.

"Make yourself at home." I gestured to the couches. "How do you feel about kebabs?"

"Fantastic," Eve said.

Seraphia nodded. "Love them."

I went to the window and set the history book on the little table. I grabbed the paper menu from the restaurant below us, then picked up a pen and pad of paper. I handed the goods off to Eve and Seraphia. "Jot down what you want."

I already knew my order by heart...and Cordelia's. I no sooner placed an order with the restaurant than Cordelia appeared, no matter where she was in the city. I swore she could hear the scratching of the pen.

Mac appeared at the door. "Ooh, good idea," she said, spotting the menu and pad of paper. "Get me a Donner Kebab, please."

"No problem."

Orders completed, I placed the paper in the bucket by the window and lowered it by the attached rope. Leaning out, I watched Berat, the restaurant owner, grab the bucket.

"Mission complete," I said, pulling my head from the window.

"That's a handy system," Seraphia said.

I grinned. "All Mac's idea. She came up with it."

Mac tore open the bag of crisps. "I'm a genius, what can I say?"

"There are bowls in the kitchen," I said. "Freshly washed, even."

Mac disappeared into the kitchen as Cordelia appeared on the windowsill, her little nose twitching. *Kebabs?*

"Yes, Cordelia."

Excellent. She trundled over to the couch and climbed up to sit between Eve and Seraphia. They must have met earlier, when Cordelia had delivered the book to Eve, because Seraphia took it in stride.

"I can't find them," Mac called.

I joined her in the kitchen and fished the bowls out of the tiny cupboard, pointing with my elbow at the little fridge. "There's some wine in there, if you want to grab it."

"Do I? It would be pure barbarism to have a girls' night without wine, even one that's aimed at solving an ancient deadly mystery and will involve—unfortunately —no drunken antics."

I grinned and filled the bowls with crisps, then took them out to the living room and handed them around. Mac joined me and passed out the mini boxes of wine, pouring Cordelia a smaller serving in a cup. Cordelia glared at her.

Mac couldn't understand Cordelia when she talked, but the look was easy to read.

"Hey, don't blame me." Mac raised her hands. "You have the lowest body weight, and I'm just doing the maths. We don't need an unconscious raccoon on our hands."

Cordelia scoffed and drank her wine.

I sipped my wine and contemplated everything we'd learned. Everything *I'd* learned since my arrival. "You know what's weird?"

"What?" Mac asked.

"There are no misfits in Guild City. Everyone

ascribes to a guild, or they get booted. No weirdos allowed."

She shrugged. "Those are the rules."

"Yeah, but there are misfits in the rest of the world. It's strange that there are none here. Seems like it should be impossible."

Mac frowned. "That's a good point."

"It's always been the way of things," Eve said. "It helps hide us and protect us if everyone has to be in a guild and follow the rules."

"But surely a few weirdos wouldn't throw off the whole magical system. I mean, they'd still have to control their signatures, right?" I asked.

"Right." Seraphia pulled her knees up to her chest. "You know, Carrow, you're right. It is very odd. We try to shove everyone into a box and stick them in a guild, but what if they don't really fit?"

"They get kicked out of town." Mac's words were a growl. "It's bloody unfair."

"Who made these rules, anyway?" I asked.

"That guy, Councilor Rasla, from the statue you saw earlier today," Seraphia said.

"The one with bird shit all over his head?" I asked.

Mac grinned. "The very same."

"So he's the one who laid the foundation of exclusion in Guild City."

"Yes." Eve sipped her wine. "Though I've never thought much of it before now. When you grow up with something, you tend to accept it and not to look too closely at it. It's just part of life."

I didn't like it. Not only because I wasn't included in a guild, but because it seemed wrong. As wrong as the cursed magic that hovered around the city wall. "Why do you think the darkness in the wall called to me?"

Mac's gaze flicked to mine. "Now, don't go thinking you're secretly evil or anything. Because you're not."

That was *exactly* what I'd been worried about. "How could you tell?"

"You're an open book, and none of the pages have been torn out."

"But I wasn't cursed."

"I have no idea why that was," Eve said. "But we'll figure it out."

"Maybe it's the magic from Orion's Heart that you absorbed," Mac said.

"Or maybe you're just a total badass," Eve added.

"Maybe." Doubtful.

A bell rang from below, catching my attention. Cordelia leapt off the couch and scampered toward the rope. She hauled on it, pulling hard to raise our dinner up the wall. I joined her and tugged the bucket up the last meter.

My mouth watered at the fragrant smell of grilled meat and spices as I lifted the bucket through the window. I handed Cordelia her little glass takeaway container, then passed around the rest of the food.

We chatted as we ate, discussing everything that we knew about the mystery. It shouldn't have been fun, but it was. At least a little. There was still the fear that hung over us, but being with Mac, Eve, and Seraphia was fun even when it was scary and tense.

Finally, we'd exhausted ourselves and every avenue of discussion. Mac yawned, and Seraphia followed suit, her mouth wide.

"You two need some rest," Eve said. "The curse is draining you."

Mac looked at Seraphia. "I've got a spare bed at my place. You can bunk there, if you want."

"Thanks. I'm exhausted." She yawned again.

I stood, my gaze going to the book that we'd brought up from Eve's shop. "Do you mind if I look at that again tonight?"

Eve frowned. "Is it safe?"

"The wall cursed them, not the book." I shrugged, trying to appear casual. "I think it will be fine. If there's a problem, Cordelia will get you."

Cordelia glared. *I need my beauty sleep.*

"You're beautiful enough, so do me a favor, okay?"

She grumbled but nodded.

"It's all yours," Seraphia said.

"Thanks." I grabbed the book and waved goodnight to them as they piled out the door.

Cordelia trundled after me to the bedroom. She slept in a ratty old armchair that Mac and I had unearthed in a secondhand shop. Mac had disapproved of our find, but I loved the worn blue velvet, and so did Cordelia.

Be quick. Cordelia climbed onto her chair. *I'll be asleep in no time.*

"Yeah, yeah." I flung myself onto the bed, barely managing to strip out of my jeans and shoes.

The night sounds of Guild City drifted through my window as I leaned back against the headboard and flipped through the pages. The golden glow of the lamp illuminated the tiny, ancient print.

What are you looking for?

"I'm not sure." I kept flipping. "I think I've got all the clues I can out of it—using my magic, at least. But I haven't read it. It's a history of Guild City."

That means it's a history of the Devil.

"Maybe." But that's exactly what I'd been thinking. I could probably learn about him through this book. Given what was growing between us, I wasn't going to look a gift book in the mouth. Even if it was cursed.

Carefully, I searched for the Devil's name. He was rarely mentioned, but when he was, he was always doing something important.

Like establishing the city, for one. Apparently, he'd been on the original council hundreds of years ago and had helped draft the city designs, basing them on his hometown of Sighișoara in Romania.

Did he miss it?

As the pages turned and the years passed, the Devil appeared more infrequently, as if he'd stepped out of the limelight and become the loner I knew him to be. For someone with so much power and influence—and so many employees—he spent most of his time alone, as far as I could tell.

Not a single friend, unless you counted Miranda. And you couldn't. She was a great right hand, but she wasn't his pal.

The mystery of the Devil—of Grey—ran through my mind as my eyelids grew heavy, and the book slipped from my grasp.

When the dream came, I didn't even realize it *was* a dream. The line between wakefulness and sleep was so fine that it didn't exist.

Instead, I was immediately in the future, wrapped around Grey as he bent over me, his fangs brushing against my skin. A shiver raced through me, fear and desire in equal parts.

I moaned, tilting my head, wanting more of him. He groaned low in his throat. The noise made the heat inside me burn ever brighter. When his fangs pierced my skin, pleasure flared.

I clutched him to me, clinging. Waves of pleasure crashed over me as he drew on my neck. Every pull felt better than the last, until my head began to spin. My heart stuttered, and my skin grew cold.

Dimly, I realized that this was bad. This wasn't normal.

"Grey." I tried to speak, but the word was barely a whisper. He didn't stop. Panic flared.

I tried to struggle, but it was too late. He'd taken too much. There wasn't enough blood left to deliver oxygen to my muscles, and I was fading away. Dying.

My last thought was one that had haunted me since I'd heard it.

Cursed Mates.

7

CARROW

Hey! Wake up!

Cold water splashed on my face, and I jerked upright, gasping.

Cordelia sat next to me on the bed, my water cup clutched in both of her little paws. She grinned toothily at me. *You weren't waking up.*

I scowled. "You hardly tried."

She held up the cup. *I tried very hard.*

"Dumping water on my face isn't trying hard." I pushed my wet hair off my forehead and tried to still my racing heart.

That dream...

I shuddered.

It couldn't be a vision of the future, could it?

But it was. It was exactly what I'd seen when I'd touched Grey last week. A vision of our future—of what "Cursed Mates" meant to us. Except we didn't know why or how, exactly.

Cordelia shifted, staring at me with solemn eyes. *The Devil is here.*

"What?" Surprise flashed through me. "Already? Why didn't you lead with that information?"

She shrugged. *I told you, didn't I?*

I groaned and climbed out of bed, still dressed in half my clothes from yesterday. "Where is he?"

In the street.

I scrubbed a hand over my face and grabbed my robe, pulling it on over my T-shirt. He didn't need to know what a slob I was. I'd been wearing this shirt for at least twenty-four hours straight.

The clock showed that it was already past two in the afternoon, yet I still felt exhausted. "How the hell did I sleep so long?"

You were up forever reading that book. The sun had already come up and everything.

I groaned, wishing I had one of those cappuccinos from the Mages' Coffeehouse. If there was one thing I needed right now, it was caffeine. Good, strong, caffeine, preferably prepared by someone else and served in a cup I wouldn't have to wash. That wasn't happening anytime soon, however.

Butterflies tumbled in my stomach as I went to the bedroom window and opened it, leaning out to look at the street below.

Just as Cordelia had said, the Devil waited down below. He was so damned handsome in the afternoon light, his suit cut impeccably to make him look like a spy out on a coffee break.

Coffee.

My gaze riveted to the two paper takeaway cups in his hands.

"Is one of those for me?" I asked.

"Indeed, it is. May I come up?"

"Did you find another copy of the book?"

"Will you let me come up if I didn't?"

"Just curious." I pointed to the drinks in his hands. "You've already got your invitation right there."

One corner of his full lips tugged up in a grin.

"Cordelia will show you in," I said. "Wait in the living room. I need a quick shower."

He nodded.

Behind me, Cordelia grumbled.

I turned to her. "I got you a kebab last night, and you owe me."

I'll do it for another kebab.

"You drive a hard bargain, madam."

She nodded. *Damn right I do. And don't think I'll forget.*

"I would never." She wouldn't let me. If I'd learned one thing, it was that Cordelia remembered what she was owed. Hell, I needed to get my business up and running so I could keep her in the lifestyle to which she'd become accustomed. No more dumpster diving for my kebab-loving raccoon.

She trundled to the door, and I darted into the bath.

The space was little and cramped, shoved under an eave that had been built hundreds of years ago. But it was mine, and I loved it. I took a shower in record time, wondering what Grey thought of my place.

By the time I'd dried and dressed in my usual black jeans and T-shirt, Cordelia was back in the bedroom. *He's waiting for you.*

"Thank you."

Kebab?

"They're not even open yet, nerd."

They are, too. It's the afternoon, not morning.

I sighed. "I'll get it later. We need to get a move on with this, and you need a more varied diet."

She scoffed and turned away to climb back onto her chair. I left her to it, heading out to join Grey in my living room. He stood by the window, his pose tense and slightly uneasy, as if he didn't know where to sit. He looked big and out of place in the tiny room.

"You can sit anywhere," I said.

He turned to me. "Thank you."

He didn't sit, instead handing me my drink.

I took it gratefully and nodded my thanks. "Is this from the mages' place?"

"Indeed. A cappuccino."

"Thank you." I sipped. "Oh, that's amazing."

He smiled, and the faintest bit of warmth entered his eyes. It made him appear almost human, although no less otherworldly in his beauty.

"So, the book?" I prodded.

"Apparently, there is another copy in the Order of Magica Archives in Chicago. My contact there, Ms. Cross, tracked it down."

"And?"

"She'll show it to us today. We are to meet her outside of the Order of the Magica's Hall of Inquiry as soon as you're ready."

"I'm ready." I grabbed my leather jacket off the back of a chair, then debated bringing the book. I didn't really want to leave it out of my sight, considering it was cursed. In and of itself, that was a valuable clue. "Let me just get the book."

He nodded, and I hurried back to my bedroom, slipping the book into the cross-body bag in which I'd been carrying it around. I returned to the living room and found him by the door.

"Ready?" he asked.

"Ready. How do we get there?"

"We'll take a portal to save on transport charms. There's one that leads directly from Guild City to Magic Side."

"Perfect."

I followed him down the stairs but paused briefly by Mac's door.

He stopped and turned back, raising a brow at me.

"I'm going to check on Mac and Seraphia." I knocked lightly, then stuck my head in. "Hello, you two. Are you all right?"

Mac and Seraphia sat at Mac's table, their heads bent over cups of tea. They looked pale and weak.

I hurried inside and dropped into a chair beside them. "You guys look like hell."

"I'm fine." Mac's voice was faintly raspy. "Eve is coming up with more of the potion that holds off the effects of this curse."

"Is she any closer to a cure?"

"Not yet."

Grey was standing in the doorway. I felt his presence like the warmth of a summer day and turned to him. "Do you have any contacts who could figure out what's wrong with them?"

"Not in town, no. But Ms. Cross may know of someone. She works at the Order, and they have access to all varieties of magic."

"Nevaeh Cross?" Seraphia asked.

"The same."

"I've heard of her. Reportedly an excellent scholar." Seraphia's face was wan. "Did she find a copy of the book?"

"She did."

"Thank fates." Seraphia's eyes brightened at the news. "I'm dying to know what history has been hidden."

"We'll find it." I turned back to Grey. "If there's someone at the Order who can help with Mac and Seraphia's condition, what will they need?"

"A hair from each of them will do." Eve's voice sounded from behind Grey. "Sorry. I was eavesdropping."

He moved aside to let her pass, and she slipped into the room. The raven followed her, its eyes as black as her dress. Her peasant-style skirt flowed around her ankles, glittering with black beads.

She handed me a bag. "Potion bombs. Your familiar let me know you were headed out on a job."

"Thank you." I took it gratefully and added it to the messenger bag with the book.

"There are scissors in the kitchen drawer," Mac said. "By the sink."

While Eve gave Seraphia and Mac more of the potions she'd concocted, I retrieved the scissors. Quickly, Mac and Seraphia each removed a tiny lock of hair.

"I hope that works," Eve said, "because I still haven't figured out what's in the curse. I'm going to the Sorcerers' Guild and Witches' Guild today to see if anyone there can help."

"Let me know if you find anything, and I'll do likewise." I gave Mac and Seraphia worried glances. "Take it easy today, okay?"

Mac saluted. "Cartoons and ice cream, no problem."

Despite the worry that still tugged at me, I laughed.

Grey and I left, and he led me toward the city gate I used most often.

"Are we headed to the Haunted Hound?" I asked.

"Yes. They have a portal that leads to Magic Side."

As I walked beside him, I couldn't help but remember the dream that had been so terrible.

"Are you all right?" he asked, noticing my silence.

"I'm fine."

We reached the pub a few minutes later, arriving at the back of the establishment.

"This way." Grey headed down the dark hallway to the main part of the pub. "The portal is in the other side of the building."

We passed in front of the bar, and I gave Quinn a wave.

"You all right?" he asked. "How are Mac and Seraphia?"

"I'm fine. They're not. We're headed to Chicago to find a cure."

"Good luck. Keep me updated."

"Will do."

He watched us with a worried expression. Grey led me down a hallway identical to the other, with shelves full of liquor bottles and an unmarked door tucked into the corner at the end.

We stepped through, and the ether sucked me and spun me through space, spitting me out in a large open square. On either side of us, skyscrapers rose toward the pale blue sky. It was earlier in the day here, the sun lower in the sky. The light glinted off the buildings and the massive lake to the north.

I heard the roar of water and felt a fine mist on my skin. I turned and gasped. Behind me, an enormous water sculpture looped overhead, floating in the air like a giant ring. Water dripped down, and a dozen screaming, happy kids played underneath.

Grey caught my momentary surprise. "That's the Rain Bridge. It's the partner of the Cloud Gate in downtown Chicago. What the humans know of as The Bean."

"Wow." I spun in a circle, taking in the city. "I've never been to America."

Grey smiled. "There are a lot of beautiful places here."

"What body of water is that?" I pointed to the glittering expanse. There was no land in the distance that I could see, but on the shore to my left, the city stretched far into the distance. "Chicago is on one of their enormous lakes, isn't it?"

"The Great Lakes. This is Lake Michigan. Magic Side sits just offshore of South Side. It resides in a pocket dimension, so it looks like water to humans."

"So only supernaturals can see it?"

"Exactly." He turned toward the street. "Come, we're not too far from Ms. Cross's office."

I followed him down the busy city street, passing supernaturals of all shapes and sizes. Unlike Guild City, which looked as ancient and magical as an old teapot shooting silver stars, Magic Side looked modern and almost normal, except for the individuals who filled the streets and the cars that rushed by.

Horns and exotic features weren't uncommon to see on passersby, and everyone's magical signatures were on display.

"They don't keep their signatures on lockdown, do they?" I asked.

Grey shook his head. "It's not required here."

"But why? Isn't their city like ours, hidden amongst humans?"

"It's similar, yes. Their rules are different. They consider it a First Amendment right."

I frowned, disliking the iron control that Guild City exerted over the magical signatures of its residents. It seemed unnecessary. Magic Side was more relaxed and still managed to thrive.

We hopped on a trolley car painted red and cream with the words *Magic Side Surface Lines* written across the side.

I looked at the rectangular windows and leather seats. "Streetcars seem a little old fashioned, don't they?"

Grey nodded. "Chicago phased out their trolley system in the '40s and '50s. Magic Side bought the old cars and kept them running. Downtown Magic Side is called the Circuit because of all the converging streetcar lines."

I nodded as I leaned against the glass. Tall buildings whipped by, though mainly, I was paying attention to the throngs of supernaturals crowding the sidewalks.

We hopped off beside a long but narrow city park.

The green oasis was dotted with pathways and benches, inviting walkers and readers to enjoy the space. There was a small, round duck pond in the center, ringed by a walkway and flower beds. On one side of the park, an enormous neoclassical building rose several stories in the air. The heavy limestone stonework was beautiful, as was the massive set of wide stairs leading up to the columned entry and massive brass doors.

"Is that the Hall of Inquiry?" I asked.

"Yes." He pulled a mobile from his pocket and typed in a message. "Ms. Cross will come get us soon."

"We can't meet her inside?"

The corner of his mouth kicked up in a small smile. "Technically, I'm not on *their* side of the law."

"You mean the legal side?"

"Precisely."

"How to you know Ms. Cross, then, if she's an Order agent?"

"I know some people in Magic Side. It's useful to

have contacts at the Order for dealing with..." He hesitated, clearly searching for the right word. "Individuals who are like me."

"You mean criminal kingpins."

He shrugged elegantly and sat down on one of the stone benches beside the pond. I took a seat beside him and watched the ducks flapping their wings at each other. "I suppose you could call them that," he said. "Chicago's magical criminal underground predates Al Capone."

"You mean gangsters? Like with Tommy guns and flappers on their arms?"

"Some might call them that, but it's a bit more complicated."

I grimaced. I'd gone a long way from Police College to associating with known criminals. "You don't deal in guns or drugs or women, do you?"

His eyes flared with surprise. "Of course not."

"Good." I believed him. Mac had told me something of the sort when we'd first talked about Grey, and in all my time knowing him and visiting his headquarters, I'd never seen anything that would turn my stomach. There were plenty of ways to circumvent magical law and make a fortune that didn't involve selling your soul.

As we waited, my mind turned back to the book I'd read last night. "You helped found Guild City."

"Yes."

"Care to give any details?"

"What do you want to know?"

I shrugged. "I'm not sure. Why aren't you on the Council anymore if you played such an important role in creating the city itself?"

"I don't want to be involved. Not anymore, at least. I served for several decades when the city was getting off the ground. Though I was never close with the other members, we agreed on most things. But the years passed, and people changed, and I lost interest."

"That was when Councilor Rasla came, right? Making the laws about the guilds and requiring everyone to join?"

He nodded. "But times were different then, and I was no longer involved."

Sadness pulled at me. "You've lost every friend you've ever had, haven't you?"

"Immortality has its downsides." He gazed into the distance. A normal person might have looked sad, but Grey looked like Grey. Cold and perfect.

Slowly, I reached for his arm.

Just a little touch, enough to see if I could feel anything in him.

"It was long ago, Carrow." He looked at my hand inching toward him, his expression knowing. "I'm fine now."

"Are you?"

Grey

Was I?

I'd been fine then, a shadow of my former self. A statue formed of ice and cold. It kept me alive. Kept me sane.

It was only with her that I'd begun to feel, to know loneliness and longing. It was bloody uncomfortable, in fact. I resisted the desire to rub my chest.

Across the courtyard, a figure appeared on the steps. Oddly, the wind whipped at her hair, though there was no breeze to be felt. She raised a hand and waved.

Ms. Nevaeh Cross.

I stood, grateful for the distraction. "We can go now."

Carrow joined me. "Is that her?"

"We'll meet her around the back of the East Wing Archives."

"Lead on."

Carrow and I strode across the park to the alley behind the building. Ms. Cross waited for us in a shady spot along the pavement, her gaze serious. She wore slim-cut trousers and a blouse that I recognized as currently fashionable. Not that I was interested in fashion, but I tried to keep up with societal changes.

Immortals—though we were rare—were notorious for being hopelessly out of date, clinging to the past. That would never be me.

"Why are you a persistent thorn in my side, Devil?" Ms. Cross fingered a fire opal pendant hanging around her neck. It glinted red with flecks of green in the sunlight.

"Thank you for your help, as always."

"You owe me. Again."

"I do." I gestured to Carrow. "Ms. Cross, this is Carrow Burton. Ms. Burton, Ms. Cross."

Ms. Cross shook Carrow's hand in the cheerful, friendly way of Americans. "Call me Neve."

Carrow flinched subtly at the touch and withdrew her hand as quickly as possible. She covered the awkward moment with a warm smile that didn't quite douse the look of concern in her eyes. "Lovely to meet you, Neve. Thank you for the help."

Had she sensed something? Most Chicagoans weren't subtle about their magical signatures, but Ms. Cross always seemed to have hers tamped down tight. I'd never known her species, and my curiosity was piqued.

Ms. Cross didn't seem to notice Carrow's reaction and gestured for us to follow. "Come on. I can sneak you in through this service entrance."

"If it's a risk, you can take me in, and Grey can stay outside," Carrow said.

Ms. Cross gave me a penetrating and perhaps slightly incriminating look. "We'll have to bend a few rules. And he has some skills that may come in handy."

She tossed us a couple of visitor badges. "I brought disguises. This is a broad-daylight infiltration. We're not going into the high-security wing, so we shouldn't raise too many eyebrows. We can be seen—just not by the wrong people, like an investigator. Or anyone who looks official. Or curious."

"So...avoid everyone but the janitors." Carrow grinned.

"Basically. Just don't draw attention to yourselves. Let me answer any questions."

Ms. Cross turned and led us through an unassuming steel door tucked into an alcove against the side of the building. She strode down a nondescript hall that was oddly narrow and short, given the imposing edifice. We followed her up a back stairwell lit with anemic industrial lights and down another long corridor. As we walked, Carrow leaned close to Ms. Cross and whispered, "I'm sorry to ask for more favors, but is there anyone here who might be able to determine what type of curse my friends have been hit with?"

Ms. Cross frowned. "Not here, necessarily, but I think I know someone. I can hook you up."

"Oh God, thank you." Carrow's voice rang with gratitude.

We were approaching an intersection when we heard a gruff female voice shouting at someone in the adjacent hall.

"Crap, that's my boss, Lieutenant Bitchface," said

Ms. Cross. "We don't want to have to answer any of her questions." She grabbed Carrow's arm and yanked her into a room, and I darted in behind them.

Two horned trolls and half a dozen imps looked up at the commotion. One of the trolls pulled off a pair of thick reading glasses and scowled at us. "Yes? Can we help you?"

There were stacks of paper everywhere, and the room was filled with a low curtain of thick smoke. Two of the imps seemed to be fighting over an elaborate abacus.

"Hi, guys," Ms. Cross said with a start. "How's the number-crunching going? I...er...am showing a few visitors around the building and wanted to show them the brains of the operation. *Arcane auditing*, I thought, and brought them here."

The troll narrowed his eyes. "This is very irregular. Who are the visitors?"

"Oh, just a couple of witnesses..." Ms. Cross stammered.

"Witnesses to what?"

"Well..." Smiling, she leaned in. "They witnessed some *serious* trespassing. On Order property, no less."

The troll scratched a horn and leaned back. "That's not normally your purview. Why are you involved?"

"Uh... this trespass involves an ancient book."

The troll grunted. "You should not bring witnesses

back here. What if they saw our work? I should report this."

Some of the imps glared at us and scooped up their precious documents. We were *non-auditors*, after all. Another growled, a clear warning that we were not to even consider taking his abacus.

Ms. Cross raised her hands in apology. "No need to file a report. We haven't seen a thing. Think of the paperwork involved. It would hold you up, and you do *important* work. I just thought it would be nice to visit."

I leaned over to catch the eyes of everyone at the table and imbued my voice with my magic. "You will not report us, gentlemen."

They blinked, and the lead troll nodded. "This visit is irregular. But I will not file a report."

"Thanks, guys. Sorry for the trouble." Ms. Cross backed toward the door and motioned for us to follow.

Once we were out, she ushered us down the hall. "Whew. That was close. Thanks for stepping in."

I raised an eyebrow. "You mentioned the book. Your cover was a bit on the nose."

"It had to be. It's nearly impossible to lie to auditors, so it's best to tell a version of the truth."

I frowned. "My apologies for all the trouble."

"Really?" she asked. "I figured you enjoyed this kind of thing—slipping in and out under your enemy's nose."

"I certainly don't hate it."

We turned the corner and crossed a skyway that led

to a large, round, colonnaded stone building with a domed top. Ms. Cross gestured to the imposing structure. "This is the archives. There is no ground-floor entrance, only an emergency exit. That's why I had to bring you through the East Wing."

Two huge wooden doors at the end of the skyway beckoned. The intricate carvings on their surface depicted scenes that constantly changed. Knights fighting dragons, scientists making discoveries, planets and nature and mathematics flashed across the doors in a whirling array.

"The different departments couldn't decide who should be represented at the entrance, so they all were," Ms. Cross said. "There were so many submissions for the artwork that they ended up squishing them all on there with magic."

"I suppose that cuts down on interdepartmental bickering," Carrow said.

"It did, though nothing keeps them quiet for long."

Carrow chuckled.

We entered the enormous domed space. The interior of the archives seemed much wider and higher than the building we had seen from the skyway. I looked down from the third-floor balcony upon which we stood, studying the chamber. The walls were lined with bookshelves, while the lower level was filled with reading desks. In the very center of the room, a large O-shaped circulation desk ringed a massive pit that descended into the earth. Imps flew down and returned with books of all shapes and sizes.

Ms. Cross gestured to the pit. "There are sixty-seven levels of stacks descending deep below Lake Michigan. It's supposed to keep the books cool. But boy, it seems like a pretty daft idea to keep an entire archive beneath the water table."

"Wow," Carrow said.

"Your book, however, is in Special Collections. It was a hassle to get access."

We followed her down the stairs into a secondary wing of the archives. It was roofed with a high glass ceiling supported by a lightweight steel framework that simultaneously contrasted with and complimented the stodgy, neoclassical limestone dome.

We were met by a three-foot-tall curator. He eyed us suspiciously as he led us into a small open-top reading cubicle. Inside, atop a large Plexiglas block, sat a single book.

The curator glared at Ms. Cross. "You are responsible for this book. I do not think that people who are not curators should be allowed to touch books like these, but I do not make the rules."

Ms. Cross smiled diplomatically. "Thank you for entrusting us with it."

The small man grumbled. "I do not trust you any farther than I can spit a tooth." He slapped a box of nitrile gloves on the table. "You do not touch the pages without gloves, or you will be evicted from the archive. You do not lick your fingers to turn the pages. You turn them gently, counting to seven as you do so. You do not sneeze on the book, or excrete any other bodily substances on the book, or you will be evicted from the archives."

He paused for a moment, and then stalked off grumbling. "I will be watching."

I approached the clear plastic box with the book. A warning label on the container read: "Hazardous: Magical Materials."

We pulled on gloves, and Ms. Cross gingerly undid the clasp and opened the case. Magic sparked around the tome, shadowy and evil, leaving an oil slick on the air.

She shuddered and held the book out. "What are you looking for, specifically?"

Carrow reached for it, but I was quicker, taking it first. She didn't need to touch something coated in magic like that. As soon as my fingertips touched the spine, I knew.

Damn it.

I could feel it, the same way I'd been able to feel it on the other book. When I flipped open the pages and saw the section that had been torn out, I wasn't surprised.

Carrow scowled. "He's been here, too."

"Who the hell did that?" Ms. Cross glared from the

book to me, and then back at the small man behind the special collections desk.

"Not us, obviously. But that's why we've come. Our copy of this book is missing the same pages."

"Could I hold it, please?" Carrow asked.

I frowned but passed it over. She took it, grimacing slightly, and ran her fingertips over the stumps of the missing pages.

Her magic flared slightly, and she scowled. "There's no new information here."

"What is your gift?" Ms. Cross asked. "And what's going on?"

"I'm a bit like a psychic or a seer, but my gift is activated by touch." Carrow handed the book back. "Whoever vandalized our book did the same thing to yours, but we have no idea who."

"There's more to it, isn't there?" Ms. Cross asked.

"A lot more, and—"

"Shh!" Ms. Cross drew our attention to the doorway.

A pair of accounting trolls had entered the room and were asking questions.

8

CARROW

Neve pressed her back against the wall of the cubicle. "Shit! Those are the trolls we walked in on earlier. I think our number is up." She looked at me. "They may not be after us, but I don't want to count on it. Do you have what you need?"

"Yes. We've got as much as we can."

"Okay, lets boogie." We backtracked through the stacks into the central chamber, hugging the shelves beneath the balconies to keep out of the sight of any possible watchers above. I followed Neve, bounding up the stairs to the second floor, and crossed over the lower half of the skyway.

Panic rose as we hurried through the corridors,

trying to avoid looking suspicious. We couldn't get caught breaking into one of the main government buildings in Magic Side. They had the manpower to hunt us down and put us behind bars, and I didn't have time to chill in a holding cell.

Mac and Seraphia didn't have time. It was up to us to save them.

I studied Neve as we turned down another one of the endless narrow corridors lined by red doors. If we got caught, it could end her career. Yet, she seemed to be having *fun*. Who was this woman, and why was she risking her job to help us?

Finally, we exited into the alley, and I heaved a sigh of relief.

It was after noon now, and the sun shone high overhead. Birds chirped from the trees in the courtyard, and Neve said, "Come on, follow me."

She led us down the sidewalk away from the Hall of Inquiry, skyscrapers to our left and the long parkway to our right. We ducked into a bar in the lower level of a century-old building. Three-paned windows let in the sun, and the bar was well lit, with high ceilings and dangling Edison bulbs. A slender, tattooed woman was working behind a granite bar top. It was trendy but quiet and cozy at the same time.

Heck yeah, this was my kind of place.

Neve flagged down the bartender and took us to a table in the corner. We seated ourselves facing the door.

"Where are we?" Grey asked.

"The Hideout." Neve indicated the name of the bar, backwards in the window, written in bold white playbill letters.

The bartender stopped next to our table. She propped on hand on her hip. "Your usual, Neve?"

"No, on the clock. Just squatting. Can you say we've been here an hour if anyone asks?"

The woman cracked a grin. "Not a problem. I'll bring you some water."

"Thanks, Diana, you're the best." Neve turned to us. "Man, I could *feel* the corrupted magic streaming off that book. Can you tell me what this is all about?"

I drew in a breath and met her penetrating gaze. I wasn't sure what to make of this woman. At first glance, she seemed unassuming, if fashionable. But there was something extremely sharp about her, a hidden intensity below the surface that I sensed when we locked gazes. I recalled the vision I'd had when I shook her hand. I'd tried to avoid it, but she'd been quick. First had been the sensation of a warm, pleasant breeze, and then my stomach had lurched as though I were plunging downward at limitless speed.

The dizziness had remained even after I'd released her hand.

I had no idea what species she was, but it didn't matter. She'd put her job on the line for us, and she deserved an explanation.

"That book is linked to something bigger in Guild City." I spoke quickly, laying out the whole story, starting from the beginning with Seraphia and the book. As I finished, Diana stopped by our table. She sat three plates of sandwiches and three glasses of water in front of us.

"What's all this?" Neve asked.

"If I know you, you've had your head stuck in a book this whole time and missed lunch. Breakfast too, probably."

"You know I'd never miss a cinnamon bun from the coffee shop." She grinned at her. "But thanks. Otherwise, you're right. I'm starving."

"Anytime, Neve."

Neve took a big bite of her sandwich and chewed, a far-off expression on her face. I bit into mine, grateful for the sustenance.

Neve swallowed. "So, you're out of leads, but you're dealing with at least three curses—one on the book and the city wall, one on Grey's memory, and one on your friends?"

Curses on everyone except me. I was grateful, but it felt weird to be the odd one out.

"The curses are linked," Grey said. "The magic feels the same, and it's all tied together. We need to know what the curse is. Then perhaps we can track whoever cast it."

Neve nodded. "Sounds like you need a Curse Diviner."

"Is that the person you mentioned earlier?" I asked. "The one who might be able to help Mac and Seraphia?"

"Yes. Fortunately for us, they don't work at the Order. We need to lay low there."

"Where are they?" Grey asked. "Who is it?"

"Madame Duvoir. She lives and works in The Dens."

Grey's face tightened. "Who does she work for?"

"The Dockside Boss," Neve said.

"Just my luck." Grey gave a wry smile. "First the Order, now this. Not that any of the others would be better."

I gave him a curious look. "What am I missing?"

"The Dens are run by the criminal underground of Magic Side," Neve said. "It's been around forever, but it really hit its stride in the 1920s."

"Gangsters," I said, remembering my earlier conversation with Grey.

"Precisely." Neve nodded. "They run a number of neighborhoods throughout Magic Side." She gave Grey a significant look. "If I remember correctly, your boy here is on their bad side."

The corner of Grey's mouth quirked up in a smile. "Not always." He looked at me. "It's an on-again, off-again business arrangement. Currently, we're off, which means we need to be careful on their turf when we speak to Madame Duvoir."

"Will she talk to us if she works for a mob boss over there?" I asked.

"For the right price," Neve said. "She's a woman who does what she wants."

"Why does the Order allow a bunch of old mobsters to control part of Magic Side?" I asked.

Neve shrugged. "Why does organized crime exist anywhere? Corruption, greed. They've got an arrangement, and we do what we can to keep everything as safe as possible. Most importantly, they make sure their goons don't start showing up and dropping spells in Mainland Chicago." She met Grey's eyes. "He'd know all about the delicate dance between crime and city."

"True enough." Grey shrugged. "The Council of Guilds can't stop me."

"That's because you own them," I said. "And you can control their minds."

"It's a handy skill."

Neve shook her head. "Well, it's not too dissimilar here. We definitely want to avoid their goons. They don't like me any more than they like you, and Carrow is an outsider, so she won't be welcome either. But I can get us in by boat once it's dark."

"By boat?" I asked.

"The Dockside Den occupies the area around the old freighter docks, which the thugs now use for whatever they want to smuggle. The Great Lakes reach the sea, you know."

I nodded, finally starting to get a more complete picture of Magic Side.

Neve finished her sandwich, leaving a bit of crust on her plate. "Ready to go find a boat?"

I ate the last bite of mine and stood. Grey joined us, laying a stack of bills on the table.

"It was on the house," Neve said. "Diana sometimes feels bad for me because of how hard I work and throws me a bone."

"Then it will be a tip." Grey turned toward the door.

I shrugged and followed him. The gesture didn't surprise me. He wasn't the type to owe anyone.

But I definitely owed him.

It took Neve the rest of the afternoon to rustle up transportation, a sleek wooden speedboat we rented off an older gentleman at the local yacht club. It cost Grey a pretty penny. By the time we were ready to depart, the sun was sinking behind the horizon. Waves gently rocked the vessel as we climbed on board.

Neve took the wheel.

From the dock, the owner scowled at us. "Be careful with her," he said.

She saluted. "You can count on me."

He grumbled and turned away, as if he couldn't bear to look.

"Can he count on you?" I asked.

Neve shrugged. "I'm not bad with driving. It's the docking that's hard."

The old man groaned. "Just bring her in slow."

"Will do, Cap." Neve pulled away from the dock and looked at the dim sky. "This timing should work well enough. The moon won't rise until a bit later, so we should have some good darkness."

Grey stood on the other side of the boat, staring out at the lake ahead. The cool breeze swept his hair back. He looked like a movie star headed to the Venice Film Festival. I'd always liked looking at those pictures in magazines—images of far-off travel I'd never get to do.

Now I was in America, and I'd been in Romania before that. My life had taken an adventurous turn.

The breeze was cool as the boat sped over small waves. Neve directed us toward the Dockside Den, looking like an expert at the wheel.

As twilight faded, I stared out at the city. It rose tall from the shore, shining skyscrapers reaching for the sky. Lights gleamed in the windows, more and more flicking on as the hour grew later.

"It's beautiful." I said.

Neve nodded. "Yes, at night. And some parts during the day. This is your first time in Magic Side?"

"Yep. It's quite different to Guild City. The people are

so open with their magic. I mean, I saw a blood sorceress striding down the street. Magic radiated off her. It was clear as day what she was. You could never be openly...powerful...like that in Guild City."

Neve shrugged. "Never been there. Heard stories, though. It doesn't make sense to me. This is a magical city. We're a magical people—it's literally who we are. Why hide our powers?"

"Except you do." The words were out of my mouth before I had time to think. Neve's jaw tightened, and I instantly regretted it.

She was silent a moment, then she spoke, not making eye contact. "It works for me."

"Sorry. I didn't mean to pry."

There was a long, awkward silence. Grey was far enough away that the wind drowned out our conversation.

"I'm still mastering my powers." I was trying to offer up something, but that didn't get any result, either. She had locked up. I continued anyway, trying to smooth the moment over. "Sometimes I just sense things. About people. Objects. I wanted to join the police, be a full detective. It didn't work out. Maybe it would have been better for me here."

Neve gave me a sympathetic look and shrugged. "This place has its own pitfalls. I've been trying to make investigator for years. Haven't managed it yet. It sounds like you have some interesting talents for it."

"None that have helped me in Guild City. I didn't have a lot of options, so I kinda had to strike out on my own—start my own detective agency."

Neve gaped. "That's amazing. Your own agency! I'm jealous. I can't imagine what it would be like to be my own boss."

I beamed a little at that. "Honestly, I'm making it up as I go along."

She smiled back. "Hey, any help you need, give me a call." She studied me for a moment, then gestured to the wheel. "Want to drive? Might as well learn some water-borne infiltration skills."

"I'm not sure the captain would approve. I haven't done it before."

She stood aside. "Nonsense. Come here."

I took her place. Beneath my palms, I felt the powerful thrum of the engines vibrating through the wheel.

Neve pointed at the controls. "Throttle up, throttle down. The wheel makes us turn to port or starboard. This button scuttles the ship, and we drown in Lake Michigan."

"What?"

She grinned. "Just kidding. Try not to hit land. You'll be fine—it's a big lake."

Handling the speedboat was exhilarating. As soon as I had got the hang of things, Neve had me punch up the engines, and we raced through the night along the dark, curving shoreline. The speedboat surged and hummed beneath my hands, begging me to go faster.

I shot a grin at Grey, then turned to Neve and shouted over the roar of the engines, "How do you know where we're going?"

"I've done this before," she yelled back.

"At night?"

"Yeah. For work."

"So, do you go into the field a lot? Hunting down bad guys?" It reminded me of my own work.

"I wish. Primarily, I'm a researcher, so they generally keep me chained to the archives." She grimaced.

"I've heard you're very good."

"Yeah, I'm so good I've been pigeonholed. They only let me out of the cage if they need me to read some ancient spell."

"Jerks."

Neve turned to look at me. "Totally. It's *really* frustrating. I do the groundwork for a lot of cases, but I'm never part of the bust."

I gently bit my lip. "Damn. That sucks."

"Yeah. I have a lot of repressed sleuthing." She grinned at me. "So what do I do? Find a healthy outlet? Noooo. I sneak a mob boss into the Order archives, then I shuttle him into the territory of another gangster. I need new hobbies."

"I'm sorry we're putting you at risk."

"Please, this is the most fun I've had all month." She

looked back. "Anyway, I'm intrigued now. I want to push the case forward. All we have to do is not get shot."

"Is the Dockside Den that dangerous?"

"Only if you aren't supposed to be there. I mean, it's a free city. In theory, we should all be able to go where we want and talk to whomever we like. Normally, I would be fine going in. They might give me a hard time because I'm a known agent, but they wouldn't mess with me too much."

"So why are we trying to slip in under cover of night?" I asked.

Neve nodded back at Grey. "He makes this a lot harder. Bosses are supposed to stay out of each other's territory. Professional courtesy and all. But since he's the one with the curse..."

Neve looked at the dark shapes looming along the shoreline. The buildings here weren't as tall, and few were lit. "Speaking of getting in the hard way, I think I'd better drive."

I gave her the wheel, and she turned down the throttle. The engines reduced to a low murmur as we puttered along the shorefront.

"Just whispers now for this last part," Neve said in a low voice. "Sound carries over water."

I quit the chitchat and watched the structures of the dockyards slip by. Their enormous, looming piers had once been used for freighters and were backed by abandoned factories and unlit warehouses. The dockside area was expansive. There were a few harbors for small boats, and a motley assortment of vessels were tied off to bobbing orange buoys further along the shore. We came to an area of old wooden docks, which led to a cluster of warehouses and tall brick buildings that lined the waterfront.

"Here we go," Neve whispered.

She cut the throttle, and we coasted silently in, sliding under the tall dock and navigating between the tall pilings. They were in bad shape, covered with crustaceans and tattered bits of old rope. Everything smelled of dead fish and something strange, like smoky tar.

Neve pointed to a piling with wooden slats nailed to it. "That's how we get up."

She secured the speedboat, tying off the bow and the stern, then turned off the engine and pocketed the keys.

By then, Grey was already at the ladder, scaling it swiftly and naturally despite his suit.

"I don't know how that man makes a suit look so appropriate for everything," she mused.

"He's like James Bond."

Neve nodded. "Yep."

I followed Grey, and Neve brought up the rear. At the top of the makeshift ladder, a small wooden hatch was propped open. Grey was already on the dock, and I shimmied through the hatch to join him.

It had begun to sprinkle lightly, a faint rain that was cool against my skin. Shipping containers towered around us, blocking our view. We tucked ourselves into the shadows as Neve joined us.

"This way," she whispered, leading us out of the maze and toward the glow of lamps.

We reached the edge of the crates, and I caught a glimpse of the dock. Gas lamps flickered gold in the darkness, their light gleaming on the puddles and glass windows of the crumbling factories along the waterfront. Wooden slats ran between us and the buildings.

Everything was brick and iron, a remnant of an industrial past that had been abandoned in this part of the city.

Something moved in the shadows.

"Guards." Neve pointed to the two men. "Those are the boss's goons. Marsh Men."

I frowned. "Marsh Men?"

"People say they came from the lake, but I don't know if it's true." Neve indicated a guard roughly twenty feet away. "I'll take that one." She crept forward, soundless and lethal. Stepping from the shadows, she called, "Yoo-hoo!"

The Marsh Man turned in surprise, but Neve was on him in seconds. She ducked a blow and spun behind him, bringing her elbow down hard on his shoulder. He dropped to his knees, and Neve followed with a swift blow to the back of his head. The guard stiffened and toppled facedown.

Neve shot me a grin. "He'll be out for a while."

"Holy crap. You move like the wind. How did you learn to do that?"

"It's Silat, a Southeast Asian martial art. A lot of law enforcement agencies use it."

To my right, Grey darted out on silent feet, his movements a blur. A moment later, I spotted him dragging the second guard into an alley between two of the old factory buildings.

"Looks like he's taken care of the other one." Neve stood. "Come on."

She sprinted across the open section of docks and disappeared into the alley where Grey had dragged the Marsh Man. I dashed after her and found Grey standing over the guard, whom he'd bound with his own belt. There were gills on the side of the guard's neck, and he glared at me with green eyes.

"The boss will have your heads for this," he said.

"He'll have to catch us first." Grey removed his tie in a sexy one-handed gesture, then crouched and gagged the Marsh Man with it. "But tell him that the Devil of Darkvale sends his regards."

"You play a risky game, Devil," Neve said.

Grey grinned. "What's life without a little risk?"

He stood and stared down the alley. "Is this the way to your Curse Diviner?"

"Madame Duvoir lives at the end." Neve hurried quietly down the road. One end of the building abutted a small Art

Deco tower, and Neve cut around to the back, where she pointed at a fire escape that hung out of reach. Grey sprang up, grabbed hold of the metal ladder, and pulled it down.

"Will she mind that we're sneaking up on her?" I asked.

"Friends' entrance," Neve said. "And she'll know we're here by now."

"The boss knows you're here as well." A feminine voice, tinged lightly with a French accent, sounded from above.

I looked up, spotting a woman with dark, curly hair and unusually bright eyes. She wore a flowing dress with long sleeves, bangles around her wrists, and a broad amber necklace. She grinned widely. "Long time no see, Neve."

"Hey, Madame Duvoir. Got some time to lend us a hand?"

"All the time in the world." She raised her brows. "You, however, will be in a world of hurt when the boss shows up."

"How long do we have?" Neve asked.

Madame Duvoir shrugged. "Well, it's Thursday, so he's down at Gigi's. The show has started, but he's already received word that there are intruders on the docks."

Us.

"So it depends on how good the show is," Madame

Duvoir said. "If it's good enough to distract him, he might just send more Marsh Men. If it's not…"

"He'll come himself." There was a slightly blood-thirsty lilt to Grey's voice. It would serve me well not to be distracted by his sophisticated manners and elegant suits. He was ruthless at heart, likely addicted to danger.

"Just come on up," Madame Duvoir said.

"You won't get in trouble?" I asked, guilt streaking through me. If the boss was so dangerous, and she worked for him…

I desperately needed her help—Mac and Seraphia needed her help—but I couldn't help worrying about her.

Madame Duvoir waved her hand. "Don't fret. I do what I want."

"Come on." Neve scaled the ladder.

I followed her, with Grey bringing up the rear.

Madame Duvoir's place was a large, open space and dimly lit, outfitted with Bohemian décor.

"This way." Madam Duvoir led us toward a round table.

We sat, and she leaned forward, eyes gleaming with interest. "So, what do you have for me?"

I pulled the book out of my bag, along with the two locks of hair. I put them on the table in front of her and told her the tale.

Her expression was impassive as she listened. When I finished, she looked at Grey. "And you're cursed, too?"

"My memory has been modified."

"Could be a spell," she said. "Not as degenerative as a curse, but it would get the job done."

"Can you determine what it is?" he asked.

"For the right price."

"Which is?"

She named a number that made my brows go up. It had more zeros than I usually saw in a year, but Grey just nodded. "It will be transferred immediately."

She pursed her lips and stared at him.

He smiled blandly and raised his wrist to his lips, speaking into his comms charm. "Miranda, could you transfer fifty thousand pounds to the account of Madame Duvoir in Magic Side, Chicago?"

"Immediately, sir."

"Excellent." Madame Duvoir said. "Everyone knows how efficient your Miranda is."

"Indeed."

"Now, let's see this book." Madam Duvoir pulled it across the table and flipped it open. She reached for the two locks of hair as well, frowning as she touched them. "You said these are cursed?"

"Yes."

"They're not cursed."

"Yes, they are." Confusion pulled at me. "Mac and Seraphia were surrounded by the same shadows that hovered around the city wall. Then they became ill."

"It's not a curse. I would feel it."

"Try harder." Frustration surged through my veins.

"Mind your manners." Madame Duvoir glared. "I'm never wrong."

"The book." Grey's tone was soothing, and he gripped my hand under the table. Gently, as if he were trying to soothe me as well.

It didn't work. Much.

But I could see his point. We needed whatever info we could get out of Madame Duvoir. I could grill her on Mac and Seraphia once we had more.

Madame Duvoir leaned over the book, studying it, absorbing it. She breathed deeply through her nose and stared at it with a dagger glare. "*This* is definitely cursed."

"But not the same curse that's on Mac and Seraphia?" I asked.

"Like I said, they aren't cursed."

It made no freaking sense, but I pressed my lips together and waited.

Madame Duvoir held out a hand to Grey. "May I?"

"Yes."

She touched his free hand, closed her eyes, and focused. "You are cursed as well. The curse is similar to the one on this book."

"And therefore, similar to the curse on the wall," Grey said. "They feel identical."

Madame Duvoir nodded. "I'm going to look into this more closely."

She rose and carried the book to a table on the far side of the room, which was covered in a variety of crystals and silver tools.

Placing the book in the center of the table, she circled it with a ring of red powder, lit two pale green candles, whispered an incantation, and blew them out. The smoke was much thicker than it should have been. Trails of it spiraled toward the book in strange patterns. Madame Duvoir turned to us, her eyes gleaming with interest. "You've got quite the problem on your hands."

I leaned toward her. "Who cast the curse?"

"That, I cannot tell you, but it was likely a sorcerer, given the type of magic. However, I do know how you can break it."

Elation surged through me. "That will save my friends."

"They're not cursed, honey."

Irritation prickled my skin, followed by the chill of fear.

Grey's grip on my hand tightened, bringing me back to myself before I snapped.

"If you can break the curse on the wall, you might learn more about your friends' situation," Madame Duvoir continued. "And you may fix the Devil's memory as well."

"You can't break the curse on my mind?" Grey asked.

"I cannot. Messing around with minds is beyond my power. But I can give you a spell to break the curse on the city wall. From there, you are likely to find more clues."

Even if that was all we'd get from her, it was still a lot.

Madame Duvoir scribbled something on a piece of paper, then collected a small bag of crystals and handed them to Grey. "These are on the house because I feel bad about your memory. You still need a few ingredients, and this spell is best cast when the moon is at its zenith."

I stared at the paper in Grey's hand. An incantation was written on it, along with instructions and a complicated drawing of swirls and spirals. But what if—

A shout sounded from below, and Neve hopped up. "Time to leave. The boss's goons are here."

"You'd better go," Madame Duvoir said. "He'll cut you apart as soon as he looks at you."

9

*G*REY

Men shouted from below us, and Madame Duvoir gestured for us to follow. "Come on," she said. "I can get you out the back way."

"Will we avoid his goons?" Ms. Cross asked.

"Most of them," Madame Duvoir said, cutting across her large flat. "Maybe not all."

I grabbed Carrow's hand, and we raced after her.

"Do you have one of those transportation charms you took off the demon back at the Crescent Hotel?" I asked Carrow.

I needed to know she had a quick and safe way out of this. I could cover her until she was through to Guild City.

"Yeah," she said. "I keep one on me, just in case."

"Won't work here," Madame Duvoir said. "The boss has this whole section blocked off. There are no easy escapes from his turf."

Clever bastard. I'd done the same at my tower.

"This way." She led us down a wide corridor.

We crept along the wooden boards, heading toward a part of the building we hadn't been in before. Outside the brick walls, I heard men running along the alley.

"Some of them know about the back exit," Madame Duvoir explained.

"We just need to get to the boat," said Ms. Cross.

The Curse Diviner muttered, "They probably know about that, too."

Ms. Cross winced. "Captain Bernard is going to be so pissed."

"I'll get him another boat," I said.

I couldn't allow her to encounter trouble on our behalf.

"If you can get to the old streetcar at the end of the dock, it will take you out of The Dens," Madame Duvoir said. "It's not technically part of the boss's holdings, so it's a safe space. Get there, and you're fine."

She hurried down a narrow spiral staircase constructed of wrought iron. I followed, my footsteps rattling against the metal. When we reached the ground floor, she gestured to a small door. "That's your out," she said. "Follow the row of buildings all the way down to the city, and you'll see the streetcar. Good luck."

I reached it first, turning back to Ms. Cross and Carrow. "I'll take out the first wave of men. You run for the streetcar."

Both women gave me skeptical looks, as if they weren't going to run while I watched their backs.

"Just be careful," I said.

"Of course," replied

Ms. Cross as she drew a wickedly curved blade from a sheath on her hip, a bloodthirsty grin on her face. The formerly reserved researcher looked ready to skin a demon alive.

"Badass." Carrow grinned.

"It's a khanjar blade from Oman. A gift from an old friend." Ms. Cross flipped the blade and caught it. "Now, let's get a move on."

Carrow reached in her bag and withdrew a potion bomb. "Courtesy of Eve."

I nodded, then turned to the door.

Madame Duvoir stepped up beside me. "Let me give you a head start."

I nodded.

She reached into the pocket of her flowing dress and withdrew a glass orb similar to Carrow's. Gray smoke swirled within the little globe. She pushed open the door and, without leaving the building, chucked the potion bomb outside.

A massive poof of dark smoke exploded upward, and men shouted from within the blinding cloud.

"Thanks." I darted out, using my superior senses to locate my targets.

I could hear them, smell them, *sense* them through the fog. I charged right, colliding with a Marsh Man. He reeked of seaweed. Strength surged through me, and I grabbed him by the collar and hurled him toward the building. He slammed into the brick and collapsed.

Behind me, Ms. Cross sprinted down the street, headed straight for a man who stood between us and the streetcar. As she neared him, she ducked low, swiping at his legs with her blade. He reached for her, but she was faster, her blade whirling with wicked grace. The knife sliced through his thighs. He screamed and toppled backward.

I heard a noise from my right and spun around. A man surged out of the darkness, his eyes gleaming red. He held up a hand that flickered with flame.

"I was hoping for a challenge," I said as he hurled the fire at me.

I took the hit, absorbing the magic as I always did with flame. He frowned and stumbled back, and I charged. My unnatural speed was impossible to avoid. There was no time to play with my prey, so I simply knocked him to the ground.

To my left, two goons tried to hit Carrow with blasts

of water. She dodged the missiles and took them out with her potion bombs. In the distance, Ms. Cross raced toward another Marsh Man.

There were more than I could count, but they were easy to find with my heightened vampire senses. The goons fought back with jets of water, swift and icy.

An icicle hit me on the side of the arm, leaving a deep gash. Dark blood seeped from the wound. But as the fog faded, I looked around to find that the three of us were alone.

"I think we're clear," Carrow said. "Let's get out of here."

"Look." Ms. Cross pointed farther down the dock.

A horde of Marsh Men raced toward us—twenty, at least.

My blood was up. Though I welcomed a second fight, I had to think of Carrow.

I couldn't risk it.

"Run," I said.

"Not without you." Carrow glared at me.

"Fine." I sprinted away from the Marsh Men, toward the streetcar.

They roared and ran faster, and I placed myself between Carrow and our pursuers. The three of us raced toward the streetcar. Idling at the end of the row of warehouses, it beckoned.

The horde pounded after us, their footsteps loud

against the wood. I looked back as several of them raised their hands. Two of them shot jets of water at us, liquid projectiles that could pierce us through.

"Dodge," I shouted.

We dove out of the way as the wave crashed to the ground behind us, then lunged up and sprinted faster. Four more Marsh Men fired water at us, but we dodged their blasts every time.

As we neared the streetcar, I looked back again. A small jet of water was shooting toward Carrow. I lunged between her and the projectile.

It slammed into my shoulder. Agony flared, and I grunted and stumbled, blood welling from the wound. I snatched a dagger from the ether and hurled it at the Marsh Man who'd attacked me.

The blade spun through the air and pierced him in the throat. The others roared with rage, but I heard only Carrow's voice:

"Grey! Come on!"

I spun and raced after them. They'd jumped onto the streetcar, and I followed, climbing on board. I turned, ready to resume the attack, but the Marsh Men had stopped and glared at us with green eyes.

"They can't get us while we're in here." Ms. Cross turned to the driver, an older woman with a wild halo of white hair. "Will this take us to the Circuit?"

"That's right, dearie. This is the express. Only four stops."

Ms. Cross nodded and slumped onto the padded seat.

The streetcar rumbled to life. Panting, I looked back at our enemies. They watched with impotent rage as the cables carried us away.

"Grey, your shoulder." Worry echoed in Carrow's voice as she moved to stand before me.

"It's fine." But it wasn't, not really. My shoulder hurt, and it should have been healed by then. Had the jet of water been laced with lethal magic? I wondered. It hadn't glowed oddly.

Ms. Cross moved to join us. "That's an ugly wound."

"Do they imbue their projectiles with anything?" I asked.

"No, it's just super-fast water."

Carrow tugged off her jacket and flipped it inside out. "I'm going to put pressure on it."

"Don't worry about me. I've had worse."

"I don't care." Gently, she pressed her jacket to the hole in my shoulder.

I sucked in air through my teeth but said nothing.

"We'll be out of The Dens soon," Ms. Cross said. "Then you can transport out of here. Or the streetcar can take you to a portal."

"How far is the portal?"

"The one in the Circuit is only a few minutes away," the driver said.

"We'll go there, thanks." Better to save the transport charm.

"Be there in five." The driver nodded. "Fast service here."

10

CARROW

As the streetcar careened through the city, I stared at Grey, worry seeming to drown me. He looked paler than usual. Weaker.

And yet, the wound wasn't that big. I'd seen him take far worse hits.

There was something different about this wound. He seemed almost...human now. Like he could die.

What if I lost him?

Fear pierced me, cold and terrible. I'd tried not to fall for him. I'd *tried.*

But I'd failed.

I swallowed hard. "You really don't think there was magic in that hit?" I asked Neve.

"I don't think so. They tend not to use that type of spell."

I nodded, looking back at Grey.

"Stop worrying," he said. "It's fine."

"We're here," the driver called as the streetcar pulled to a stop.

Thank God. I gazed at the large open courtyard and spinning water wheel, grateful to see our exit. Neve helped me get Grey to the portal. He was able to walk on his own, but he was unusually weak.

The ether sucked us in and spit us out at the Haunted Hound. We stood in the dark corridor to catch our breath.

Quinn appeared at the entrance. Concern was etched across his strong features. "Carrow? What's wrong?"

"Nothing." I trusted Quinn, but the Devil didn't. He was inexplicably feeling low, and I didn't want to draw attention to that fact.

All the same, the vampire's shoulders straightened. "We're fine."

There wasn't the slightest hint in his voice that he was hurt.

"All right. Let me know if you need anything." Quinn melted into the shadows of the bar, leaving me alone.

I turned to Grey, worry twisting inside me. "You really aren't okay."

"I'm *fine*."

"Fine is a weak word."

"I'm not healing as well as I normally might, but we'll get to the bottom of it." His expression was bland and calm, reassuring.

I didn't buy it for a minute.

I tilted my head to reveal my neck. "Drink my blood. It worked last time."

"No." His voice cracked like a whip. "Absolutely not."

"Just a little. It will help. It always does."

"You know what might happen if I drink your blood."

A vision of my dream flickered in front of my mind. *Cursed Mates.*

"We'll do it at your place. You have the self-control, I know it. And it'll heal you."

"Not even there. I want it too badly, and once I start..."

He wouldn't be able to stop.

He didn't say it, but he didn't have to. I could read the fear in him clearly.

"It will never happen," he said. "Thank you, but forget it."

"Fine, then we're getting a healer." I prayed it would help.

"Excellent plan."

I nodded and took his arm. "Let's go."

We switched to the other abandoned hallway and took the portal back to Guild City, staggering through the streets to his place. It was after midnight, and the pavement bustled with people going from bar to bar, shouting and laughing. Shops glittered with life and magic, but I had no interest in them.

By the time we reached the Devil's tower, even I was feeling drained. The two security guards at the front hopped to attention, their movements gracefully powerful in the way of all shifters. They swung open the doors, and we entered, finding Miranda at her station.

Concern creased her brow. "Devil? What's wrong?"

"Everything is fine, Miranda." His voice sounded normal, but his face was so pale. "Don't concern yourself."

"Could you get the healer?" I asked.

She nodded, her gaze moving between us. "He's having a drink in the bar, in fact."

I frowned. "How many drinks?"

"He hasn't been here long enough to lose his head. I'll send him to your quarters, Devil."

Grey nodded, and we headed in that direction. Fortunately, there was no one in the halls between the lobby and his flat. The healer was already there, waiting for us. He was slightly red in the face, as if he'd run the whole way, and I wondered what Miranda had told him.

"Thank you for coming, Doratio," Grey said.

The old healer nodded, his pale green eyes glinting with concern. "But of course."

Grey unlocked the charm that protected his flat and let us in.

The healer's white cloak swept around him as he entered. "What happened?" he asked.

"We were fighting some Marsh Men in Magic Side, Chicago," I said. "They shot Grey with a jet of water. I think it was enchanted because he hasn't been able to heal like normal."

The healer frowned. "That is strange, indeed." He gestured to a chair by the window that looked out on the beach. "Sit, please."

Grey sat. His face was impassive, though his shoulder slowly seeped blood. It had to hurt, but other than the faint paleness of his features, he showed no sign of pain.

I paced anxiously as Doratio knelt by his chair to inspect the gash. He hovered his hand over the shoulder wound, then the arm wound, his magic flaring. In the reflection of the glass, I could see his brow crease with concern.

"I feel no magic here," he said. "These wounds are clean, made only by water moving fast enough to cut."

Shit. Something really was different about this. "Then why isn't he healing?"

"That, I do not know."

Something was different about Grey. That had to be it. Why else would his healing ability suddenly just *stop*?

A sense of foreboding threatened to drag me down.

"Can you heal it in your normal fashion?" Grey asked.

"Yes, yes. Though I'm afraid I can't restore your vampire healing ability."

Grey nodded. "See to the wounds. I'll sort that out."

Anxiously, I watched the healer feed his power into Grey's body. The gashes knitted themselves back together in front of my eyes, though Grey's skin was still pale.

"That's the best I can do." The healer stood and turned to me. "And you, my dear? Do you need treatment?"

"No." Grey had got between me and any hits I might have taken, so I was fine.

"Then I'll be on my way." He turned and went to the door, disappearing silently into the night. I had to assume he had an arrangement to bill Miranda.

Grey turned to me, rising. "Are you all right?"

I nodded, my gaze meeting his. "I'm fine. Just worried about you."

"Don't be."

"I can't help it." I cared about him. As much as we both knew it was a bad idea, I couldn't help the feelings that were threatening to overwhelm me.

Somehow, over the last week, I was coming close to falling for him.

He opened his mouth, something unreadable flickering in his eyes. Then he closed it, swallowing the words. When he spoke, his words had nothing to do with us. "We need to gather this collection of ingredients."

I nodded. "Of course. I'd like to check in with Eve as well. See how Mac is doing."

"I'm going to call Miranda and give her the list."

"Tell her to consult with Eve."

My friend sold certain magical ingredients. The least I could do was try to push a little business her way. She'd already done the same for me.

He nodded.

I moved to the side of the room, closer to the window so that I could have some privacy for my call. I dialed Eve, waiting impatiently as the phone rang.

Finally, she picked up.

"How are they doing?" I asked.

"Stable, but only because of the potion I've brewed. It won't last forever, though." She sounded worried. "Have you found out the nature of their curse?"

"The Curse Diviner said they weren't cursed at all."

"What? Impossible."

"Not according to her."

"Then what's wrong with them?"

"She didn't know. She thinks it may be related to the curse on the city wall, so if we break that, it may help them."

"But *how*? That doesn't make any sense."

"I've no idea, but it's the only lead I have."

"Damn it." Eve's voice trailed off. "I don't know how to fix them. Or how much longer they've got."

"Let's follow the advice of the Curse Diviner," I said. "And I can have Grey send you a healer for Mac and Seraphia."

"That might help, thanks."

I nodded, spotting Miranda's reflection in the window. She'd arrived to take the list of ingredients from Grey. "And Eve? Miranda may be stopping by to get some things to help us break the curse on the wall. We can attempt to cast the spell tomorrow near midnight."

"All right. I'll be on the lookout."

We hung up, and I turned to Grey and Miranda. "Can you send the healer to Eve's place? Maybe he can help Mac and Seraphia."

Grey nodded. "Of course." He turned to Miranda. "See that it is done."

She nodded and raised the list. "I'll let you know how I get on with these. Dinner should be here any moment."

"Thank you." Grey held the door for her, and she disappeared silently from the room. He looked at me. "You're worried for your friends."

"Of course."

"We'll find a way to fix them, I swear it."

We couldn't even find a way to fix *us*, but I didn't say it.

A knock sounded a moment later. When Grey

answered it, a man stood in the door with a pizza in hand.

Grey accepted the box from the man and shut the door.

"Pizza?" I asked.

"Doesn't everyone like pizza?"

"Even immortal vampires, it seems." My stomach growled.

"Let's eat." He took the food to the table near the window, then went through a doorway that I'd never used. "Would you like a beer?"

"Yes, please." I opened the pizza box and inhaled the aroma. Delicious.

Grey walked back to the table with two frosty beer bottles in his hands. He was the best-looking thing I'd ever seen.

I took mine gratefully and sat, then grabbed a slice of pizza. Grey joined me and clinked his beer bottle against mine.

"To your friends," he said. "We'll find a way to heal them."

"To Mac and Seraphia."

We ate in comfortable silence. It should have been like a date. Pizza and beer and a beautiful view.

Instead, it was weird as hell. Not so much the energy with him, but the threat that hung over us. It tugged at me, making me anxious and worried.

"Miranda will let us know soon about the ingredients," he said, clearly trying to calm my nerves by reminding me of our forward progress on our problems.

"Yeah. Great." I looked at the clock, shocked to see that it was nearly four a.m. The time change from Chicago had thrown us all off. "I should head home."

"Sleep here tonight. In the spare room."

I swallowed hard, wanting to take him up on his offer, yet knowing it was a bad idea.

"It's an entirely separate room," he said. "And it will save you travel time."

"That would be helpful." And I was exhausted. "Do you mind if I get a shower?" I'd stayed in an en suite bedroom the last time.

"Of course."

"Thanks." I polished off the last of my pizza and stood, grabbing the beer that I hadn't finished. "I'll see you in the morning."

He nodded. "Thank you for your help tonight."

"No, thank you." I turned and all but ran for the bedroom, disappearing into the quiet silence.

The shower was divine, as it had been last time. I finished off the beer while standing beneath the hot spray, replaying the day in my head. By the time I stepped out, I was clean, but no more relaxed. Despite the late hour, the idea of sleep was absurd right now. I was too keyed up. Too worried.

Maybe a book would help.

I put my clothes back on and went to the door,

listening carefully for any sign of movement in the living room. There was none, so I peeked my head out.

Silence.

Grey must have gone to his room.

I strode into the living room and went to the bookshelf, feeling like I was poking around his private space.

I was, actually.

And I *did* want a book . . . but not as badly as I wanted a look at his collection.

Honestly, I was snooping.

But it was just books, so it didn't seem so bad.

The collection was varied, and this was only part of it. There was an enormous bookshelf in his bedroom, too. Novels, nonfiction, and a surprisingly large assortment of poetry. I reached for one that looked well-worn and gasped at the vision that popped into my head:

Grey, reading alone.

It was a lonely sight rather than cozy. I couldn't tell if he actually *felt* lonely in the vision, but it sure looked that way. I put the book back and reached for another.

A similar vision shot into my mind. I went down the line of the bookshelf, running my fingertips over the spines. Grey's clothes changed each time, flashing from past to present depending on when he had read the book.

So many years.

Alone.

That was the thing about immortality. You were

constantly alone. Even if you found someone, they died eventually, leaving you alone. Again.

From what I understood of my new world, heavens and hells were real. They were called afterlives, and almost all supernaturals went to one when they died. What you believed in life would determine where you went in death, so it wasn't really an end.

Except for Grey and the other immortals. They stayed on earth forever. Alone.

Tears pricked my eyes.

"Exploring?" Grey's low voice sounded from the corner.

I jumped, gasping. Slowly, I turned, the book clutched in my hand. He wore simple charcoal sleep pants and a T-shirt, looking more casual and handsome than I'd ever seen him. I swallowed hard. "I...uh... couldn't sleep."

"Looking for reading material?"

"Yeah."

"That's a good one." He nodded to the book in my hand. "Does your gift work on it?"

"It does, but I didn't come out here to snoop."

He raised his eyebrows, clearly not buying it.

"Well, not entirely."

A smile tugged up at the corner of his mouth. "See anything interesting?"

"You, reading a lot of books."

"Helps the time pass."

"You don't hate being immortal?"

"Hate?" He frowned. "I don't know if I hate it. This is just the way life is."

"It sounds terribly lonely." I wanted to hug him.

He turned and strode to the window, as if he didn't want to consider the idea. Finally, he said, "I'm used to it."

"I'm worried about you." About his health, but also about this. About the fortress he'd locked himself inside for so long.

"You don't need to be."

"On the contrary, I believe she should be." The voice sounded from behind us, and I turned, my heart in my throat.

The air on the other side of the room shimmered, and the Oracle appeared out of thin air.

"Oracle?" Grey frowned. "Can't you knock?"

"Not for this."

"Have you learned something?"

I looked at him, eyebrows raised in question.

"I asked her to look into our Cursed Mate situation," he explained.

The Oracle approached, her semi-transparent form shimmering in the light. She was beautiful, with delicate features and long hair. Her dress flowed around her like water, and her movements were as graceful as gentle waves on the shore.

She stopped in front of Grey, staring up at him with

interest gleaming in her eyes. I moved around her to make sure I could see them both, unease prickling my skin.

"You are different," the Oracle said.

"What?" he asked.

"I haven't been able to see much regarding your issue, but you've changed recently. It's unlocked something in my vision, and..."

She hesitated, and anticipation sparked across my skin. *Speak!* I wanted to scream.

She held her hand over his chest. "May I?"

He nodded.

When she laid her hand on his chest, magic glittered in the air, and an icy wind that forebode something terrible whipped around us.

Finally, she spoke. "You are mortal now."

What the hell?

"Mortal?" Surprised flashed in his voice.

"You've felt different lately, correct?"

"I have."

Her gaze flickered over him. "You have lost your healing ability."

He nodded. "Yes. Anything else?"

She sighed heavily. "If I am right, time is going to catch up with you very, very soon. That is the nature of your curse."

"Time?" I asked. "What do you mean?"

"The Devil's time is almost up. He's been alive over five hundred years, but now that he has found his Cursed Mate, it has ignited a change in him. The immortality is seeping away, and he will pay the price of living for so many years."

"What the hell does that mean?" Grey asked.

"Soon, you will cross over to an afterworld. I give it a few weeks, maybe a month. But do not fret—you might go to a nice place, if you are lucky."

"After all the things I've done?" he scoffed. "It'll be hell for me."

She shrugged. "Maybe, though you're a different man than you were when you committed those atrocities. Perhaps you've done enough good to earn a better afterlife."

His lips twisted. "Doubtful."

Panic threatened to suffocate me. They were talking about him going to hell. Casually, like he was going to the shop to pick up a loaf of bread.

We'd *just* found one another, and he was about to be torn away? Sent to an afterlife while I was left here on earth? I'd just realized I cared for him, and now we were going to be forced apart?

I moved into the Oracle's line of sight. "Why did this happen?"

"Because of you, my dear. You're his mate, decreed by fate. But he is a turned vampire, immortal and everlasting. Until he found you, at least. Until he bit you."

"How do we fix it?" I demanded, anxiety screaming within me.

"That's the cursed part of this entire situation, I'm afraid. You are the one who started the transition for him, and you will be the one to end it."

"No," Grey snapped, shocking me.

I stared at him. "Of course I'll help end it."

"You can't, Carrow." The expression in his eyes gentled as he looked at me. "You know what must be done to stop this. You've seen it."

The dream flashed through my mind.

He'd drink me to death.

"That's it," he said, clearly seeing that I understood. He turned to the Oracle. "The only way to stop this is for me to drain her, isn't it?"

"Yes. Her blood heals you. *All* of her blood will return your immortality."

Fear scrabbled inside me like an animal in a cage. I desperately reached for solutions. "What if he just drinks a little, but more often? Daily or weekly? Would that work?"

11

GREY

My heartbeat thundered in my head as I stared at Carrow.

She was willing to let me drink from her at regular intervals to keep my miserable life. The beast inside me roared, wanting to claw its way to the surface.

Survive.

I swallowed hard, clenching my fists. If we tried that, the beast would win. I could still taste her blood on my tongue. Still feel the warmth of her beneath me, hear her moans in my ear. If we tried that again, I would never stop. The beast would rise. It wouldn't stop at small amounts meant to keep me mortal. It would want it all—it would want immortality.

"No." I tried to keep my voice gentle.

Instead, I wanted to rage. This wasn't how anything was supposed to happen. I'd been in control for so long, and suddenly, it was all slipping away.

I looked at the Oracle. "How long do I have, precisely?"

"Like I said...three weeks? A month? Time is calling you, and it will be too strong to resist soon. If an injury doesn't take you first."

"This is crazy." Carrow strode away, then back, pacing with restless energy. "Fate has decreed that we are meant to be together, but it would tear us apart. No happily ever after, no matter what."

"You know that would never happen, anyway," I said.

She jerked back, a hurt expression crossing her face, and self-loathing streaked through me. "What? I'm not good enough for you? You don't care for me at all?"

The beast inside me roared, this time with anger. It wanted her as much as I did, and that was the problem.

"I have a solution," Carrow said. "Yet you're ignoring it. My blood heals you. Therefore, it can keep you alive if you only take a little."

"It won't work, dear," the Oracle said. "The beast inside him would never stop. If he gets a taste of you, it is all over."

"I don't believe that," she said.

"Well, you should." My voice was hard. "For some

insane reason, you believe that I'm a good person. But there are parts of me that you do not know."

She scowled. "It feels like you're giving up."

"I'm not. If there is a way to stop this, I'll find it." Until I'd met Carrow, I might not have even fought my fate.

Bloody hell, I was lying to myself. Of course I'd have fought it. I was an animal and always had been. Going easily into that good night would never be in my nature, even if I didn't much like my present.

With Carrow, I very much liked my present.

More than liked it, in fact. Going to hell after finding her? It'd be worse than torture.

"I'll be leaving." The Oracle drifted away, becoming more transparent.

"If you discover anything, let me know," I said. "Anything at all."

She nodded and disappeared.

Carrow stared at me, her face white. "Why are you being so stubborn?"

I moved toward her, unable to help myself. Gently, I gripped her arms. "You don't understand the thing inside me. The monster that I truly am."

"You have control."

"I do, yes. Until I taste your blood. Last time, it took everything I had to stop. And now that the beast senses our end...it will fight harder."

"You speak of it as if it's not yourself."

"I shouldn't. Because it *is* me." I shook my head, images floating in front of my mind. "The things I did in my past..."

"That was a long time ago. Hundreds of years ago, when you were still a victim of the blood lust that takes new vampires."

"It is no excuse. And the beast...that's my way of thinking of the actions as not my own. Yet they were."

"You're different now."

"Maybe, but not different enough." My gaze traced her features. I wanted to kiss her. Desperately. "You should go."

"No."

"It's safer." I drew her scent into my lungs, unable to help myself. "Aren't you afraid?"

"Never." Sadness flickered in her eyes. "Our plan to not fall for each other was pointless."

"Fate doesn't care about our plans, I'm afraid. This wheel is already turning and will continue to turn."

"Then it doesn't matter what we do." She leaned up and kissed me. Wrapping her arms around my neck, she pressed against me. Her form was long and lean, softness and strength.

It was the best damned thing I'd ever felt.

I groaned, unable to help myself, and took her in my arms, kissing her as if my life depended on it, careful to keep my fangs in check. I couldn't taste even a drop of her blood, not with the beast ready to rise at the slightest notice.

"I want you," she moaned, moving her lips to my neck. She kissed a path down the skin there, sending fire flicking through my veins with every press of her lips.

I tilted my head, giving her better access. When her tongue swiped across my skin, warm and hot, a shudder ran through me.

It'd been years since I'd felt anything this good. Since I'd wanted anything like this.

Only with Carrow.

I ran my hands down her slim waist, pulling her closer to me. Greedily, I gripped her full hips and picked her up. She wrapped her legs around me, pressing her heat against my stomach. Again, I shuddered.

There was no way I could resist this.

"Carrow, I want you." The words were torn from my throat. "More than anything."

"Yes." She kissed me hard. "Yes. Now."

I carried her toward my bedroom, heart pounding.

If we were going to be damned, then we would have this. It didn't matter if we fell for each other or not—our fate was determined. So damn it, we would have each other tonight.

I reached the bed and lowered her down, trying to treat her as delicately as she deserved. She fisted my shirt, pulling me on top of her.

Her thighs were parted, and I fit perfectly between

them. She moaned and arched her back, running her hands over my shoulders and down to my waist.

I yanked my shirt over my head, desperate to feel her hands on my bare skin. Desperate to touch every part of her. Quickly, she tugged her shirt off, taking with it the simple bra beneath.

My gaze riveted to her breasts. "Beautiful."

She ran her hands over my shoulders, pulling me closer against her. My hips fit perfectly in the V between her legs, and she began to move against me, seeking friction. The pleasure made my breath catch in my throat. I gripped her thighs, drawing away.

In a few swift movements, I had her jeans off. Then her underwear. The sight of her took my breath. I knelt between her thighs, my knees on the floor, and looked up at her. "May I?"

Eyes wide, she nodded, her golden hair glinting in the light.

I bent my head to her, tasting her. A groan rumbled up through my chest, impossible to stop. Her taste and scent surrounded me, and I fell into it.

Heaven.

It wasn't long until she was shuddering beneath me, crying out in a way that made me desperate to sink inside of her.

She pulled at my shoulders. "Now, Grey. Please, now."

I rose, divesting myself of the rest of my clothing as she watched. She dragged me on top of her, the heat of her skin making me dizzy.

A thought tugged, dread uncoiling. "I don't have protection for you."

"I'm on birth control." She wrapped her legs around me, her warmth sending a shudder through me. "Please. Now."

I hadn't been with a woman in centuries, so there wasn't a risk giving Carrow something unsavory.

"Are you sure?" It took everything in me to hold back.

"Yes." She arched against me, and I groaned.

My resistance crumbled. Her heat and warmth were such a contrast to my cold life, and I'd never wanted anything so badly in all the centuries I'd been alive.

Our bodies joined, and pleasure exploded. It stole through me until there was nothing but the two of us. Together.

Carrow

I woke with the sun on my face and delightfully sore muscles. The bed was empty but not cold. A robe had been laid out for me. I pulled it on, the smooth fabric gliding like water over my skin. It had to be silk.

I found Grey in the living room, a tray of coffee and muffins in front of him.

"Grey," I began, "about last night—"

He looked up, his icy eyes flashing. "We can't discuss last night."

"Um—"

"I can't, Carrow."

I blinked at him, confused by the quick about-face. It had been amazing, and he couldn't even talk about it?

He rose, shoulders tense but eyes soft. As ever, he walked with lethal grace as he approached me. "I will say only this. It was the best night of my miserable existence. But if I can't have it again—which I can't, because there is no future in which both of us survive—I do not have the strength to discuss it."

"Um..." I was completely at a loss for words.

A knock sounded at the door.

The smile he gave me was small but genuine. Sad, too. Then he turned to answer. "That should be Miranda. She'll have the ingredients we requested."

He opened the door. As expected, Miranda stood there, along with Eve. Her raven was nowhere to be seen, but she was dressed entirely in dark purple leather that matched her hair.

"Please come in," Grey said.

The two women entered. Miranda carried a bag to the table and emptied the contents onto the surface.

Grey sat at the table. While he inspected the small bottles, I went to stand at Eve's side. "How are Mac and Seraphia?"

"Stable, still. They feel like shit, but they're doing all right."

I nodded, my heart thundering. We joined Grey and Miranda, and I poured us all coffee.

Miranda took it with a grateful nod. "We were able to get everything but the Powderwort and Devonian."

"I didn't have either," Eve said, "and I don't think you can find them in town."

I took a big gulp of the coffee, not minding that it was hot. I needed something to get my head together. Everything was going off the rails.

"I know where to get the Devonian," Grey said.

My gaze flicked to him. That was good. I turned to Eve. "That leaves the Powderwort. Any clues?"

"Yes, in fact. There's a supplier in human London."

"A supernatural, of course?" Miranda asked.

"Yes. An old friend." Eve raised her brows at me. "Do you want to help me find it?"

I looked at Grey.

"Go with her." His voice was firm, as if he didn't want me to argue.

After what we'd learned last night, I didn't particularly want to be parted from him. But it was reasonable.

And smart. I wasn't in love with him, for God's sake. I cared for him—more deeply than I wanted to admit. But it would do neither of us any good to fall for the other.

"I'll take care of the Devonian," Grey said. "You get the Powderwort. With any luck, we can meet back here before midnight."

"Well before midnight," Eve said. "I saw what the spell required, and we'll need time to set up for it."

Grey nodded.

I stood, still holding my coffee cup. "I'll change really quick."

Eve rose. "I'll come with you."

We went into the bedroom where I'd left my things after my shower last night.

Eve closed the door and gave me a searching look. "You seem different."

"Um, yeah."

"Spill."

"We need to get the Powderwort."

"Not dressed like that." She eyed the silk robe. "You can talk and dress at the same time. I know you've got it in you."

I scowled at her but did as she said, spilling the whole sad, terrible tale as I pulled on my clothes.

Eve sat down hard on a chair. "Oh, fates, that's bad."

"Yeah, very bad."

She swallowed hard, her eyes dark. "Listen to him, Carrow. If the Devil says it's too dangerous for him to bite you, believe him. He knows his strength better than you do."

"He'd never hurt me."

"He wouldn't want to." She shook her head. "That's why he's saying no to your plan. *And* the Oracle confirmed it wouldn't work. You've got to listen to him."

I shook my head. "Let's talk about this later."

"Avoiding it won't change the answer."

I ignored her and went to the living room, finding it empty. Grey was likely in his room, changing. I didn't want to leave without seeing him, but I couldn't march in there like we were a couple and kiss him goodbye.

"I'll see you later," I called.

"Be careful." His voice echoed through the door, and I turned away, heart twisting.

"Come on," Eve said.

We hurried out of Grey's place. By now, I'd learned the layout of the halls so well that even the disorientation spell didn't work on me. Miranda wasn't at her hostess stand—probably doing something far more important—and the man who stood in her place just nodded goodbye to us.

The day was rainy and gray again, and I pulled up the collar of my jacket as we stepped outside. "It's like the weather knows things are going tits up."

Eve squeezed my hand. "Don't worry. We've got this."

"Are we going through the Haunted Hound?"

"Yeah."

I nodded and followed her down the nearly empty street. A few brave shoppers were out, fighting with their umbrellas as the wind picked up. At one point, her raven joined us, but I didn't mention it. By the time we reached the gatehouse that led to the Haunted Hound, I was unpleasantly damp.

We passed through the gate, and the ether shoved us out into the darkened hallway at the back of the Haunted Hound. Eve led the way to the main part of the bar, but instead of turning right to go toward Quinn, she went left, heading for the roaring fire.

I joined her, spotting the ghostly dog who lay curled up in front of the flames, snoring away. "What are we doing over here?"

"Drying out." She spun around in front of the fire, sighing with pleasure. "It won't last long, since we're headed right back into it, but I couldn't resist." She gestured for me to join her. "Come on."

I stepped up beside her, sighing in pleasure as the warmth hit my chilled skin. In seconds, my clothes were perfectly dry, even my boots and socks. "Wow, that's amazing."

"A nice little spell." She tugged on her jacket to straighten it, then started toward the bar. "Come on, let's get out into London and get this over with."

I followed her, cutting between the tables, which were full with the late morning crowd. Pots of tea nestled against pints of beer as the various supernaturals chatted and read the newspaper.

From behind the bar, Quinn smiled at us. "Anything I can get you, ladies?"

"An umbrella?" I asked.

"You're in luck." He bent down and retrieved two from the shelf below the bar, one bright yellow and the other blue. As we took them with gratitude,

he leaned toward Eve, concern on his face. "How are Mac and Seraphia?"

"Hanging in there. We think we have a bit of a lead."

He nodded. "Then don't let me hold you up."

"Thanks, Quinn." I raised my umbrella in salute, then followed Eve out the door.

As in Guild City, it was raining in London. The gray sky shed not a single ray of sunlight on all of Covent Garden.

I popped open my blue umbrella, looking up to see the image of the Cookie Monster staring down at me. Eve's umbrella had Big Bird on it. Despite myself, I laughed, then looked at Eve. "Where to?"

"The Thames."

"Somewhere in particular?" I asked, hoping to avoid a soggy march.

"My friend lives on a narrowboat," she explained. "On a mooring at Battersea."

I made a face and pulled out my mobile. "Bit of a trip from here. Hold on, let me check the map..."

"Lead on."

Together, we hurried toward the Underground, clattering down the stairs and out of the rain. Quickly, I bought us tickets, since I no longer carried my Oyster Card. Less than a month ago, I'd been a regular Londoner with no idea that magic existed. Now my return to the Tube felt old-school, familiar yet foreign.

Eve's raven followed us, drawing stares from the humans. We crowded onto the train with the rest of the passengers, and I counted the stops as we made our way to our destination. Finally, we reached our stop, and we flowed out with the other passengers and up the stairs, back into the rain. A short walk later, we caught a bus, which deposited us relatively close to the water.

I led Eve down the street toward the Thames. The river was sluggish and brown today, traveling slowly toward the sea. I pointed to the private docks crowded with the long, low boats popular in the south of England. "Do you know which one?"

She stepped up to the railing, trying to get her bearings. "I think so. Come on."

She led the way to the docks, bypassing the sign that made it clear that only owners and visitors were welcome.

The wooden pier bobbed underfoot as we walked. About half the boats were empty—their occupants were at work, I imagined—but the others gleamed with light.

"I can't believe people live on these," Eve said. "Including the man we're visiting."

"That's pretty freaking cool." Something splashed in the river beside the dock, spraying me with cold water. "Damp, though."

"*Way* too damp." Eve led me to the end of the landing, where a boat strung with fairy lights bobbed—perhaps an odd touch for the morning but welcome on that gray day. The craft was long and low like its neighbors, built of a gleaming brown wood that was varnished to within an inch of its life. Plants in little pots grew on the top.

The back of the boat was flat, with a steering wheel and a U-shaped bench situated around a table. A man lounged on the bench, his handsome features lit by the white lights above him. He looked like a poet—long, lean form, angled face, and full lips. His dark hair fell over his brow and he watched us with gleaming obsidian eyes.

He looked like James Dean or some other rock-star poet with dark eyes and full lips who watched you from the shadows. If my heart weren't half wrapped up in Grey, I'd have given him a second look.

As it was, Grey was the only one I could think of. He'd fit himself into my heart and mind in a way with which I wasn't fully comfortable, especially after the revelations of last night.

I shook the thoughts away and returned my attention to the man.

Behind him, the city buildings rose tall into the thick clouds. Golden lights sparkled in the windows, a magical backdrop for the narrowboat.

"Eve." His voice was smooth as whiskey with a burn at the back end, and he didn't rise. "Been a while."

"Hey, Xavier." Eve's voice was strangely tight and breathless.

I looked at her. The slightest hint of a flush rose to her cheeks, and she shifted. Her raven sat on one of the boats behind her, almost blending into the scenery. Xavier glanced at the raven, confusion flickering in his eyes, then back at Eve. Her flush seemed to deepen.

I grinned. There had definitely been something here.

Xavier's gaze moved to me. "Hello, new girl."

"I'm Carrow." I didn't step forward to offer him my hand.

Xavier rose with a long, lean grace. "What can I help you with? Because I assume it's not me you've come to see, Eve."

"You're correct." Eve's voice had regained its usual tone. "We're here to see Michael."

Xavier's brows rose. "Michael, is it?"

"We need some ingredients," she said. "And if you could take us, we'd appreciate it."

"For a price, of course."

I reached for my pocket, but he shook his head. "Not money, new girl."

"Then what?" I asked.

"You're the one with the familiar, the raccoon?"

"Cordelia?"

"That's the one."

"How do you know about Cordelia?"

"Not many raccoons in London." He shrugged. "And that one gets around. I have a job for your Cordelia."

"You'll have to take it up with her." My mind was already spinning with ways to bribe the raccoon.

"You'll put in a good word for me?" he asked.

"Yeah, of course."

"Now?"

My eyebrows rose. "What, you don't trust me?"

He grinned and shrugged, his movements so graceful that he might have been a ballet dancer. "I trust one person: my brother. And that's it."

"Would that be Michael?" I asked.

"That's the one. Now, about Cordelia?"

"Sure. I'll see if I can get her here," I said. "She doesn't always come when I call."

"Promise her a kebab," Eve suggested.

I nodded and met Xavier's gaze. "Just a hint—you'll get better work out of her if you bribe her."

The corner of his lips tugged up in a grin. "All right. Thanks."

I called Cordelia with my mind. *Come on, dude, get over here. I need some help.*

A moment later, Cordelia appeared on the dock behind me, her teeth bared and her fighting face on full display.

"Not that kind of help," I said.

She looked up at me, frowning. *Then what's the rush?*

I gestured to the poet. "Xavier needs your help with something. And if you help him, then he'll help me."

She shifted to sit upright on her butt and stared at him. *What does he want? Does he know I work for kebabs?*

I looked at him. "Can you understand her?"

"No. But it's a thieving job."

I like thieving.

"She's interested." I frowned, my former cop self not quite liking the sound of this. "But who would she be stealing from?"

"No one good, that's for sure," Xavier said.

Strangely enough, I believed him. "Is it dangerous?"

He shrugged. "Not more so than anything else. I need her to sneak into a club through a back alley and retrieve something."

I can do it. Cordelia looked at me. *We'll have to talk terms, though. Kebab terms.*

I nodded at her, wondering where the hell my life had gone off the tracks. I was the intermediary between a man and a raccoon as they discussed payment for theft. Not what I'd imagined for my life.

This was ten times better.

"She's agreed to it," I said. "Can we work it out after you help us?"

Xavier nodded, his gaze moving briefly to Eve, then away. "Sure. Come aboard. We can deal with payment next week."

"Thanks." I stepped onto the boat, feeling like I was venturing into a whole new world.

12

CARROW

The narrowboat rocked underfoot as I moved closer to Xavier. Eve and Cordelia joined us, and he gestured to the bench. "Have a seat, and we'll be on our way."

We sat, and he moved gracefully around the boat, untying it from its moorings and turning it on. The fog had grown thicker over the river, but he piloted expertly away from the small marina and out into the wide expanse of the Thames.

I leaned closer to Eve and whispered. "You have a history with this guy?"

"Not one that I'm going to discuss right now."

"Fair enough." I leaned back and looked out at the

city, trying to see it through the fog. It was nearly impossible. The thick gray stuff obscured everything.

Xavier seemed to know where he was going, though I couldn't see any kind of radar. He stared off into the distance, turning the big wooden wheel slightly to keep us on track.

The current was stronger in the middle of the river, hurrying twigs and leaves along. In the depths, I could see golden sparkles shooting through the dark water. Small splashes rose to the surface, seeming to come from deep within the river.

"What's in there?" I asked.

"Things you can't imagine," Xavier said.

I groaned. "Come on, you can't do that. Details, man."

His mouth quirked. "Fine. Magical fish. Maybe a sea monster, depending on the season. Definitely some water fae. Possibly my ex-boyfriend."

"He get on the wrong side of someone?" I asked.

"Yeah. Me."

My eyebrows shot up, but Xavier chuckled. "Don't worry. I didn't have him offed in the river, so don't go spreading that around. Absolutely no mob ties here."

"Sure." I didn't know much about a magical London mob—it was probably in Guild City. Hell, Grey was probably the mob.

Which made me realize that I had no idea what kind of supernatural this guy was. His physical form didn't reveal anything. I couldn't see his ears, but maybe they were pointed. He could be fae like Eve. He had the same ethereal beauty.

"You're staring," Eve whispered.

"Oops."

"I don't mind," Xavier said. "Beautiful women staring at me isn't a problem."

Shit.

My cheeks heated. He had exceptional hearing, but I still had no idea what he was.

In the distance, a shadow appeared in the middle of the river. As we neared, I realized it was a little island. A small thatched-roof cottage sat in the middle, a single building on the speck of land. Roses climbed up the stone walls, and a little green field surrounded it. Two sheep chewed busily at the grass, and they looked up at us, blinking sleepily. A barrier of brambles surrounded the island like a wall, and a little wooden dock sat at one side.

"So sweet it makes your teeth ache, doesn't it?" Xavier asked.

The charming little house looked like it had been taken right out of the Cotswolds and plunked down in the middle of the Thames. "That's one way to put it." I frowned. "But don't the humans think it's odd? Or can they not see it because of magic?"

"The second one," said Xavier.

"What about the other boats? Won't they ram into it? It's in the middle of the river."

"They're magically diverted around it. It's not a problem." He pulled up to the wooden dock and leapt out, tying off the boat to two metal cleats.

"Why does he live all the way out here?" I asked Eve.

"He likes it."

"Not Guild City?"

"He doesn't have a guild," Xavier said. "Neither do I, for that matter."

He didn't sound at all bitter about it, but I couldn't imagine living out here alone. Xavier's lifestyle I could imagine. Barge life seemed cool, but this...it seemed cold and lonely.

I definitely needed to get my shit sorted with the Council, because I did *not* want to end up booted out of Guild City and living on a cold, wet island in the middle of the Thames, no matter how charming the house was.

The door of the pretty cottage opened, and an enormous man stepped out. He was well over six feet tall, with the broad shoulders and the strong legs of an athlete. His warm complexion was the opposite of his brother's pale one, as were his strong jaw and bright green eyes.

He reminded me of Quinn—a handsome, wholesome-looking man who played rugby on the weekends and went down to the pub to watch the football with his boys.

His eyes searched us keenly as he wiped his big hands on the canvas apron he wore around his waist. His broad shoulders strained against his soft, dark T-shirt.

Next to me, Cordelia leaned against my leg as if swooning. *I like him.*

He was good looking, all right. Both the brothers were in totally different ways.

"What have you brought me, Xavier?" His voice was a low, soft rumble. Somehow, I was certain that he'd never raised it in his life.

"Just some visitors." Xavier grinned cheekily and sat back down on the bench in his boat, lacing his fingers together behind his neck. "I'll leave you to it."

"Those will kill you." Disapproval echoed in Michael's voice.

"Thanks, Mom." Xavier gave him a beatific smile and took a drag.

The sound of chickens squawking from the back made Cordelia stand up straight, her little eyes bright. *I'm going to go pay them a visit.*

"Don't eat them," I said.

Sure, sure. She scampered off, moving quickly around the cottage to the back.

"They can handle themselves against the likes of her." Michael looked between the two of us. "If you're here, then you know who I am. Who are you?"

"I'm Eve," my companion said.

His brows went up as if he recognized the name, and his gaze flicked to Xavier, who still sat behind us. "Nice to meet you, Eve."

"And I'm Carrow," I offered.

"Ah, Carrow. The new girl in Guild City?" The words held no hint of dislike. I was impressed. Clearly, he didn't hold a grudge about not living there or being in a guild.

If they booted me, I doubted I'd be able to say the same.

I nodded. "Yeah. That's me."

"Why don't you come in?" Without waiting for an answer, he turned and strolled into his house.

We followed, leaving Xavier outside.

The interior was far larger than the exterior made it look, with ancient stone walls and a gleaming wooden floor. The main entry room was sparsely decorated, but he led us to a cozy kitchen at the back. A fire burned on the hearth, and herbs hung from the ceiling, drying in the warmth.

It was a cluttered, homey space, with bottles of ingredients lying next to bread and fruit—as if he mixed work and life seamlessly.

"Cup of tea?" he asked.

We were in a hurry, but it would be downright rude to say no. And my bones were cold from the ride over. "That'd be lovely, thanks."

He nodded and put the kettle on. It boiled almost

instantaneously, and I grinned. "Is that magic that makes it go so fast?"

"Best spell I ever learned." He removed the kettle and made the tea, then brought the mugs over to the table.

The surface was covered with the tools of his trade—everything from silver knives to powdered leaves—and he nodded at the clutter. "Shove some of that over, will you?"

"Sure thing." Gingerly, I arranged things out of the way, not sure what was dangerous or valuable.

Eve helped, moving more quickly, clearly more comfortable with the items on the table.

Michael put the cups down and sat, and we joined him.

"What is it that you need?" he asked.

"We need some Powderwort," Eve said. "And as far as I know, you're the best place to get it in town."

"The only place."

"That, too." She sipped her tea. "Oh, this is good."

"My own blend."

"Do you have the Powderwort?" I asked. "Two of our friends have been cursed, and we're hoping it will help."

He frowned. "Doesn't work on people."

"I know," Eve said. "The curse is on a wall, but it's spread to them. We're hoping that if we fix the wall, there will be a spillover effect."

"Hmm." Doubt flashed in his eyes, but he nodded. "All right. I can give you some. But you'll have to earn it."

"How?" I asked.

He nodded toward Eve. "I already know what I want from her. Like for like."

"Potions?" she asked.

"Yes. Fae ones. Ones I cannot make."

"That's fine. Which?"

"Heart's Own Arrow and Believer Draft."

I looked at Eve, wondering if she knew what those were. From the look in her eyes, she did. And she was curious.

Come on, ask him why he wants them.

She didn't, unfortunately.

His gaze turned to me, and I stuffed the info aside for later. I wanted to know what those potions did and why he wanted them.

"As for you..." He tapped his chin, clearly thinking.

"I don't have a ton of control over my magic, but I'm getting better."

"Yes. I heard what you did for Guild City."

"I'm afraid I probably can't save any more cities, if that's what you're after."

He chuckled. "Indeed, no. But I do have a request." He stood. "Will you follow me?"

I rose with a mournful glance at my tea.

"Bring it with you," he said.

"Thanks. It's chilly out there." I grabbed the tea, and Eve did the same.

We followed him through the house, passing through a cozy room that looked like a small library.

He led us out a back door. Cordelia sat on a stone bench, staring longingly at some chickens. They glared back at her, and I left them to it, my gaze drawn by a beautiful old well.

He gestured to it. "This goes somewhere. Not the Thames, but I don't know where."

I walked toward it and leaned over, careful not to touch it as I stared down into the darkness. Magic filtered from the depths, sparkling and strange.

"Has it always been here?" Eve asked. "Or did it suddenly appear?"

"Came with the property." Michael joined me, leaning over to look down into the darkness. "I'd like you to see if you can tell me where it goes."

"I don't have to go in there, do I?" I shivered.

"I wouldn't advise it, no. The magical signature changes from day to day. Right now, it's all right. Sometimes, though, it's bloody awful. Other times, it takes all I've got not to jump right in."

"Jump in?"

"It's like there are sirens down there, calling me or something."

"That's freaking dangerous," I said.

"You're telling me. Can you do it?"

"I can try."

"Thank you." He nodded and stepped back.

I handed my teacup to Eve, and she and Michael joined Cordelia on the bench. The raccoon seemed annoyed at the interruption of her private time with the chickens but kept her snout shut.

I turned my attention to the well. Drawing in a deep breath, I hovered my hands over the stone wall surrounding it.

I'd been practicing lately and was a hell of a lot better. This was totally doable.

And no pressure. It wasn't like my friends' lives were hanging in the balance or anything.

Show me where you go.

Magic sparked through me, and I drew it to the surface as Grey had shown me. As my power flowed through my veins, I pressed my hands to the stone wall.

Show me where you go.

Power blasted into me, and I was nearly blown backward. I stiffened my spine and held on tight. Gasping, I squeezed my eyes shut and tried to see what the well was trying to show me.

All was darkness.

Come on.

Something beckoned from the blackness behind my eyelids. I sent my consciousness toward it and, suddenly, I was falling. The wind tore at my hair, and my scream was lost on the wind.

Down I went, farther and farther.

Horrified, I realized that I was falling into the well. I hadn't moved a muscle, but my magic was pulling me into the depths of the dark hole and whatever waited there.

The wind slowed as gravity weakened, and I began to float. I found my footing. Head spinning, I opened my eyes.

Fields stretched before me, massive hills and valleys that spanned hundreds of miles. I spun in a circle, searching for anything recognizable.

Was I really here?

At my feet, a brilliant pink wildflower wobbled in the breeze. I bent to touch it, to test my theory.

My hand passed through it.

"Bloody hell." I stood, spinning again.

In the distance, I spotted a stone circle, stark amongst the green hills. Beyond the circle was a blue ocean, sparkling and bright, but there was no one here, and not a hint of what this place could be. It was almost too beautiful, too pure to be real.

I could explore, but that would take time I didn't have. And who knew what I would find? What if I lost my way, lost my connection with my body?

It was too risky. I'd bring back what information I could and hope it was enough. I tried to get my mobile out of my pocket to snap a picture, but the device didn't work.

Carefully, I counted the stones in the stone circle, memorizing their shapes and patterns. I memorized the flowers around me, the number of hills, the scent on the air, and the sound of the birds calling in the distance.

When I'd collected as much data as I could, I closed my eyes and envisioned being in my body. It took a few tries—enough that fear began to drive my heartbeat—but eventually, I felt myself flying upward, the wind tearing at my hair once more.

I returned to consciousness in my body with a sensation like I was being weighed down by a ton of bricks. To my relief, the heavy feeling disappeared, and I felt...normal.

I opened my eyes.

"Well?" Eve said. "Did you see anything?"

"Did you see me fall into the well?" I asked.

"Nope. You stood there like a statue."

I nodded. "Good. Can we go inside? Do you have pen and paper?"

"Yes." Michael hopped up, eagerness on his face.

I followed him into the kitchen, where he furnished me with writing implements. Quickly, I sketched everything I'd seen, describing it all as I went.

"Did you see a woman there?" he asked, leaning forward, his gaze intense.

"I didn't." I frowned. "Should I have?"

"Um..." He shook his head, leaning back. "I heard her, but it could have been my imagination."

Oh, *that* was interesting. This was a mystery I'd like to know more about. And it had been good practice. I'd sent my consciousness somewhere else. It hadn't been a vision. This time, I'd *gone* there. A bit like when I'd used my power in the hotel room in Romania and zoomed around through the vision of Mariketta's tomb, but more intense.

I was getting stronger, and this might be the perfect place to practice. "I need to go help my friends, but I could come back and look again, if you like. See if I can find her without you having to go into the well."

He nodded. "That would be lovely, thank you. I'm quite keen to go in, but everyone knows that enchanted wells are dangerous."

"Of course." I nodded as if I'd known that all along.

He rose. "Thank you for the help. Give me a moment, and I'll have that Powderwort for you."

He left the room, and Eve leaned toward me. "Your magic did something different, didn't it?"

"I'm getting more powerful. I think I might have projected my consciousness somewhere else."

Her brow rose. "Astral projection? That's rare, even for supernaturals."

"That's what it felt like."

"Nicely done."

Michael returned with a small bag and handed it to Eve. "Best of luck with your friends."

She thanked him, and we said our goodbyes. As we

left, I glanced back at Michael. The big man stood outside of his cottage, looking out of place and perfectly at ease at the same time.

"Ready?" Xavier's voice drew my attention.

I turned to the poet. "Yeah. Let's get out of here."

13

The Devonian had been a pain in the arse to acquire, but the task had given me time to think.

My fate was set, but Carrow's wasn't. I could use the time I had left—before hell claimed me—to make sure that she was set up well for the future. No matter what I did, however, I couldn't fall for her any more than I already had.

Easier said than done

Fortunately, I'd managed to meet everyone at the edge of the clearing at the assigned time. The sun was low in the horizon, and the sky was alight with a fiery sunset that made the world glow.

My gaze sought out Carrow. She stood next to Eve

and Quinn. Eve was showing them a large piece of paper. She pointed, speaking. Mac and Seraphia sat on a broken old bench near the wall. They looked exhausted and pale, their eyes darkly shadowed.

Worry twisted inside me, an entirely unfamiliar feeling. Absently, I rubbed my chest.

Was this what becoming mortal felt like?

Bloody awful.

Carrow spotted me, and a smile broke out across her face.

Warmth flowed through me, no longer quite so unexpected and strange. I shook it off, tightening my grip on the small jar of Devonian, and strode over to join them.

"Did you get it?" Carrow asked.

"Yes." I held it up.

Eve folded up the paper and tucked it in her pocket. She held out her hand. "Excellent. Shouldn't take me long to make the potion."

"Eve is going to perform the spell," Carrow said. "She's the most qualified, given her line of work."

I nodded and handed her the jar. "Thank you."

"No problem." Eve took the Devonian and went to join Mac and Seraphia. A small cauldron was set up on the end of their bench. Quinn joined them, but Carrow stayed at my side, her shoulder inches from mine. I could sense the heat of her, and I clenched my fists, resisting the desire to touch her.

"How are you feeling?" she asked.

"Fine."

"Are you sure?"

"One hundred percent." It *did* feel different being mortal, if I were willing to admit it. Which I wasn't. Not to her, at least. She didn't deserve that burden.

"I wish you'd consider what I offered," she said.

Her blood. Regularly. My heart raced. "No. Even if I did, you heard what the Oracle said. It's impossible."

"We'll find a way to fix this, Grey. I swear it."

I nodded, though I didn't believe it. Wouldn't even cast my mind in that direction. I hadn't known hope in so long that I couldn't conceive it. She'd walked into my life, changing everything. Now, with my fate spelled out for me, that hope had been yanked away.

I wouldn't seek it again.

I'd been alone in life, and I would be alone in the afterlife. It was fate.

I'd do what was necessary and keep moving forward, but hope was lost to me.

"Almost done," Eve called. The cauldron in front of her smoked a pale yellow, giving off a scent of hay and flowers. There was no visible flame, but fae magic was unfamiliar to me. Maybe she didn't need fire for brewing potions.

We watched in silence, though I desperately wanted to speak more to Carrow. Now wasn't the time, however, and I didn't know what to say, anyway.

Finally, Eve stood, the cauldron in her hands. Because she'd used no flame to brew the potion, it was cool enough to touch. It glowed, illuminating her face with a pale golden light.

She handed the cauldron to Quinn, who held it like it was his firstborn, carefully and securely. A bull could charge him, and he wouldn't drop it.

Eve pulled the paper out of her pocket and unfolded it. It showed a detailed drawing of the wall and the ground in front of it. Symbols had been sketched over both, parts of the spell that I recognized.

"We're going to need to paint the potion onto the wall and ground," Eve said. "But it's a complicated design. It'll take ages if I try to do it alone, and we don't have that kind of time." She glanced up, as if looking for the moon, which was slowly rising. It was full dark already, and the streetlamps were burning.

"We'll help," Carrow said. "But I should paint the wall. Mac and Seraphia became cursed when they got too close to the wall. I was immune, though."

"I'll take a brush, too," I said.

"But—"

"My days are numbered anyway, Carrow. The least I can do is help with this."

She frowned, pain flashing in her eyes. Eve looked at me, bemused, but I didn't elaborate. She was smart enough not to ask.

"Thanks." Eve carefully tore the map into four

sections, then handed them around, skipping Mac and Seraphia but keeping one for herself. She went to the bench and gathered pots and slender brushes. She handed them around, then filled the little pots with the potion that she'd made. "Do your best to replicate the design as you see it on the paper."

I nodded and took mine, then met Carrow's gaze.

"This is like art class for the damned," she said.

I chuckled.

"Come on." Eve got to work.

Carrow and I headed straight for the stone wall, while Eve and Quinn stopped in the courtyard.

Eve frowned at it. "This grass is a problem."

As I began to paint the symbol on the stones, Eve knelt and pressed her hand to the ground. Her magic flared briefly, and the grass began to wilt. The flowers shriveled and died until there was nothing but dirt and gravel for the first ten meters in front of the wall.

"That's better." Eve looked at Quinn. "Do your best to paint the potion onto the dirt. Drip it, if you must. We need to get the symbols in place for the spell to have something to grip onto."

Carrow and I stopped in front of the wall and looked at each other.

"Your eyes are glowing green again," I said.

"It's something about this wall and this curse." She frowned at me. "The dark curse isn't getting you, though. Not the way it got Mac and Seraphia."

"Thank fates for small favors, maybe." I tried to smile, but it felt unnatural. I turned to the wall and began to paint.

Together, the four of us worked. The paint glowed with magic as we drew the symbols, and I could feel the pulsing evil in the wall.

"Can you sense it?" Carrow asked. "Whatever is polluting this place?"

"I do. Feels like it's been here a long time. Like it's grown roots."

"But it's still not getting to you, is it?" Worry echoed in her voice, and her paintbrush stilled as she looked at me. "Not the way it got to Mac and Seraphia?"

"I'm fine."

She frowned but didn't press me. We returned to our work, and I couldn't help but steal glances at her. Every now and again, I caught her looking back—sometimes at her friends, sometimes at the statue of Councilor Rasla, a frown twisting her lips.

"You don't like him," I said.

"I don't like what I've learned of him."

"He was a bastard," I said. "But long dead now, thank fates. Stuck in his afterlife."

Like I soon would be.

The morbid thought turned my stomach, and I refocused on the wall. The moon continued to rise, and the hour grew late.

"How is everyone coming?" Eve asked. "We're running out of time."

Carrow

I looked up at the moon, which was reaching its zenith. Eve was right—the moon was climbing.

My shoulder ached from holding the paintbrush upright for so long, but I pushed on, looking down at the directions she'd given me. I was no artist, but I'd replicated it pretty well. The paint glowed and pulsed with magic, giving me hope that this would work.

Finally, we were done.

I stepped back to admire my handiwork. Grey's looked better than mine, but the designs on the ground were a bit of a disaster. Eve and Quinn had been required to paint the potion over gravel and dirt, which was nearly impossible to do.

Eve tilted her head as she stared down at it. "I know it looks like hell, but I think it will get the job done. It's just meant to provide a conduit for the spell."

"Are you ready to cast it?" Grey asked.

Eve nodded and pulled the paper out of her pocket. The four of us lined up at the edge of the painted ground. I could feel Mac's and Seraphia's hopeful gazes on us as Eve began to recite the words.

I looked down at the paper she was reading. The spell was fairly long and complicated, a series of words in a language I didn't recognize.

Eve's voice carried at first, but soon began to trail off. I looked at her, concerned.

She frowned back at me, panic in her eyes. "My throat is tightening up when I try to read the words. Like the spell won't let me."

I took the paper. "Let me try."

The words were unrecognizable, but they came easily to my tongue. As I read them, power began to flicker all around, the painted lines glowing ever brighter. The words came ever more smoothly, and anxiety tightened in my chest.

Why was this so easy for me?

What was it about this evil place that called to me so? Was it the power of Orion's Heart that I'd absorbed? Had it made me evil, as I'd feared?

No.

I couldn't be dragged down by fear. Not when we were so close. Not when Mac's and Seraphia's lives hung in the balance.

The magic in the potion pulsed more strongly, making the air vibrate. It shook my muscles, and it took everything I had to remain on my feet. Eve braced herself against Quinn, and Grey gripped my shoulders to steady me as the ground trembled.

A low roar swept through the clearing, as if the wind were waking.

"Maybe you should stop." Eve's voice trembled from the sheer force of the air that vibrated all around us.

No. I couldn't.

I had to keep going. The building called to me. The spell called to me.

The roaring grew louder, the wind whipping my hair back from my face. My eyes watered, and I squinted at the words, barely able to see them through the tears.

They swam into focus, and I kept going, my voice rising.

"Stop," Eve shouted.

"It's too dangerous," Quinn said.

I ignored them. Nothing could make me stop now.

It began to pour, massive waves of water coming from the sky. Thunder boomed, and lightning cracked.

"Eve, I think—"

Grey's words were cut off by a blast of power that blew him back from me. I remained standing as the dark magic washed over me in a mushroom cloud, rolling out from the wall. As it passed by, the force of the power shriveled the words in my throat.

I staggered, my vision going blind.

The screaming wind reached a terrible crescendo, then died. The rain stopped. The wind ceased.

Gasping, I blinked.

My vision returned, and I realized that I was staring straight up at the sky.

I was lying on the ground.

Holy hell, I'd fallen over and not even noticed. My muscles ached as I dragged myself upright, the gravel biting into my palms.

Blearily, I took stock of my situation. My back was to the wall. Across the courtyard, I spotted Mac and Seraphia, both collapsed on the bench. The others lay scattered between them and me.

Panic flared. I scrambled to my feet and raced toward my friends, fear screaming inside me.

I fell to my knees beside them, anxiously searching them for signs of life.

"Mac! Seraphia!" I shook their shoulders. "Are you okay?"

Mac coughed and sat up, her face pale and her eyes shadowed. "I'm fine."

Slowly, Seraphia joined her. She rubbed her face with a shaking hand, her gaze meeting mine. "Is it done?"

"I think so. Do you feel better?"

"Um...not really?"

Mac looked over my shoulder, her gaze widening. "Holy fates. Look at that."

A chill raced over me as I turned.

The wall was gone.

In its place stood a ramshackle tower. The building was ancient and beautiful, though in ill repair. Large glass windows overlooked the abandoned courtyard, and the stone was a fine, pale gray.

"That's been there all along." Awe filled me as I stood. "Just hidden."

"Look at Councilor Rasla." Mac's voice was soft.

I turned to find his statue glowing with a faint light.

"Right before the wave of magic hit us, some of it rushed into him," Mac said.

I stared at the statue, but my attention was dragged back to the building. It called to me so fiercely that I couldn't resist it. My skin vibrated with awareness as I walked toward it, curiosity pulling me.

Mac joined me, her steps slow. She wasn't better yet. I could feel that as well as I could feel the pull from the tower. Seraphia joined us.

I stopped about five meters away from it. "What's going on here?"

"I have no idea," Mac said. "But it pulls at me."

"Me, too," Seraphia said.

Eve joined us, her expression grave. "I had no idea this building was here." She turned to look at Grey, who had stood. "Did you know about this?"

He stared at it, jaw tight and eyes shadowed. "No. But I must have. I played a role in determining the positioning of all guild towers, and yet...this one is gone from my memory."

"Hidden by whoever cursed you." I continued toward the building, desperate to touch it.

Mac and Seraphia stuck by my side, seemingly as compelled as I was. The stone walls and glittering glass called to me. The massive wooden door was a beacon that beckoned me.

"Stop!" Eve said. "Don't go any closer. There's still dark magic there. We didn't get rid of all of it."

I swallowed hard, trying without success to fight the pull. "There are answers in there. Why didn't the spell work to break the curse?"

"It worked, partially," Quinn said. He joined Mac and gripped her arm, forcing her to stop approaching the tower. She struggled but was too weak to fight him. "It cursed you, Mac. You shouldn't go any closer."

"He's right." I was nearly there now, my attention half captured by the stone and glass structure. "Same for Seraphia."

Eve grabbed Seraphia, stopping her from going any closer. Grey approached me, but I shook my head. "It didn't curse me before. I'll be fine. And we need to know what this place is. Why didn't the spell work fully?"

I could still feel the dark magic radiating from it.

"Maybe there's something inside that is powering the spell," Eve said. "If we could get in and destroy it, we could stop it."

That made sense. I pressed on, reaching the front door. My skin tingled with awareness as I stared at it.

So close.

I was so close to something, but I had no idea what. This tower appeared haunted, the magic that surrounded it steeped in history and evil.

And yet...

I was drawn to it.

Was *I* evil? Had Orion's Stone turned *me*?

"Are you sure about this?" Grey stood close to my side, his voice low.

"I am." Trembling, I raised my hand. "I need to know."

I reached for the door and tried to open it. It didn't budge. A forcefield prickled against my fingers, burning.

"It's shielded," I said. "No way to get in. Probably not even through a window."

Next to me, Grey bent down and picked up a large rock. He looked at me, a question in his eyes.

I nodded. "Try it."

He stepped back and hurled the rock at one of the lower windows. When it reached the glass, the rock exploded into a thousand tiny fragments.

"We won't try to break in by force, then." I allowed my magic to flow toward the surface, calling upon my gift.

What are you? What is this curse that darkens your stone and stains your glass?

My fingertips pressed to the wooden door, and a

shock of awareness raced up my arms. My questions went unanswered.

Why is this tower cursed?

Information blasted into my head. Images flashed— Black Church, an office, scattered papers, books, a man.

Ubhan.

The sorcerer on the Council.

The knowledge hit me like a ton of stone, so hard that pain flashed through my mind, and blackness took me.

14

The Devil

Carrow went limp, and her knees buckled. I swept her into my arms before she could fall, my heart thundering. She hung limply, unconscious.

"What's wrong with her?" Panic sounded in Eve's voice.

"I don't know." I cradled her against me as I awkwardly reached around to feel for her pulse, fear chilling me. I found the steady beat thudding beneath her skin. "She's alive, thank fates."

"We're closest to the Haunted Hound," Quinn said. "Let's go there. I have something that could help revive her."

I nodded, turning to hurry toward the gate that

would lead to the pub. Quinn and Eve helped Mac and Seraphia, and we reached the gate a few minutes later. I strode through first, determined to get Carrow to safety. She felt so fragile in my arms that it made worry twist my insides.

The ether depositing us in the darkened hallway of the Haunted Hound. I marched into the main part of the pub, noticing the half-dozen patrons lingering over their pints. I glared at them. "Leave."

Every single one of them leapt to their feet and rushed out into the night. The bartender—a woman I didn't recognize—glared at me.

Quinn stepped up beside me. "Now, was that necessary?"

"I don't know, but it felt good." I carried Carrow toward the large armchairs by the roaring fire and set her down in one of them.

The ghostly hound lying in front of the flames lifted his head to blink sleepily at us. I ignored the beast. Kneeling at Carrow's side, I gently patted her pale cheek. "Carrow, wake up."

Eve, Mac, and Seraphia joined us, the two cursed women taking other chairs. Cordelia appeared a moment later, sitting on the floor at the base of Carrow's chair. Concern gleamed in her dark eyes. *I felt it happen. Is she all right?*

"I don't know."

Cordelia twisted her little paws and climbed up next

to Carrow on the chair. Squeezing her fluffy bulk onto the seat, she stared up at her.

Quinn appeared a moment later, a small vial in his hands. He uncorked it and handed it to me. "Smelling salts."

The fumes were enough to make my eyes water, and I gently wafted it under Carrow's nose as Cordelia cringed away.

Carrow gasped and sat upright, smacking the salts away from her face. She looked around, her expression confused and eyes frantic. "What happened?"

"You passed out at the tower," I said.

Everyone hovered around, staring at her in concern.

She blinked, her expression calming a bit. "I remember. I remember." She rubbed her head, squeezing her eyes shut. "Just let me think."

The bartender came up with a tray of beers and set them on the small table by one of the chairs. "You look like you could use these."

"Thanks, Kate," Quinn said. "Do we have any sandwiches left from earlier?"

She nodded. "I'll bring them out."

Carrow's eyes flickered open. "It's the sorcerers."

"The sorcerers?" I frowned. "Just like Madame Duvoir said."

"Exactly." Carrow nodded. "She said that the curse could only be placed by a sorcerer, and I saw Ubhan's office in Black Church when I asked what had cursed the building."

"*He* did it?" Seraphia's eyes widened. "But he's on the Council."

"Exactly. They're up to their eyeballs in secrets," Mac said. "And this cursed tower is one of them."

"But the tower was cursed before Ubhan was born," Eve said. "Otherwise, we'd remember it."

"I don't know how he is involved, but he is." Carrow rubbed her arms. "If we want to break the curse on the tower, we need to get into his office and find out what, exactly, is going on."

Can't we just blow up the tower if it's such a problem?

I looked at the little raccoon. "Not advisable."

She looked at Carrow, clearly hoping to get a different answer.

"What he said." Carrow looked at me. "It's midnight. Now would be a good time to break into his office."

"Ubhan is notorious for working nights," Eve said. "He's called the Owl of Black Church because he's always swooping around in the dark, being creepy at odd hours."

"So he could be there right now." Carrow frowned.

"Let me make a call." I stood. "Perhaps I can find a good time to break in."

Carrow nodded, and I strode across the room, raising the comms charm on my wrist to my lips. "Miranda?"

"Yes?" She answered immediately.

"Will you check the schedules at Black Church? I need to know a good time to try to get into Councilor Ubhan's office."

"Yes, just a moment."

I waited while she consulted our sources. We had access to private council information, and while we might not know everything that went on in the meetings, we at least knew when those meetings would be held.

She returned a few minutes later. "An official from Glasgow is coming tomorrow morning. They'll all be in the main meeting room then. Apparently, it's a big deal."

"Perfect, thank you." I cut the connection and returned to the group by the fire.

They seemed exhausted as they sipped their beers. Carrow looked up at me. "Well?"

"Tomorrow morning." I relayed Miranda's information.

"It's for the best," Eve said. "We need to rest."

Carrow leaned toward Mac and Seraphia. "How do you feel?"

"A little better, maybe," Mac said. "But weird, too."

"Like I'm pulled toward that tower," Seraphia said.

"Exactly." Mac nodded emphatically.

"Me, too." Carrow frowned. "But I'm not cursed like you guys."

"It's strange," Eve said. "But I think I might feel it,

too." She laughed dryly. "Maybe I'm just easily influenced."

"Why is this all happening now?" Seraphia asked. "I believe the pages were torn out of the book long ago. And that tower was *definitely* hidden long ago. There's no way that it was done anytime within the living memory of the residents." She looked at me. "Begging your pardon."

I nodded. "Your point is sound, though. Whoever did it could erase my memory, but not that of the whole town."

"As for why it's happening now..." Carrow's face was pale. "Maybe it's me. I'm the new one here. Maybe I triggered it somehow. Perhaps with Orion's Stone."

"There's no known connection right now," Quinn said. "This isn't your fault. More likely, this is something Ubhan has done."

Carrow opened her mouth to protest, but Mac cut her off. "I agree. You're going to fix this. It's not your fault."

Eve leaned forward. "Tomorrow, we'll find the answers in Ubhan's office. There's got to be something there that tells us how to finish breaking the curse."

Carrow nodded, worry still in her eyes. I reached out to touch her but pulled my hand back at the last second. We needed to keep our distance. Now, especially.

Carrow

The next morning after a night in my own bed—alone —I waited at a café table tucked behind a vine-covered trellis. My coffee sat before me, untouched, and the newspaper I held went unread. The morning sun beat down brightly, and I watched Black Church for any sign of movement.

The massive building sat on the other side of the square, and I'd chosen a table at one of the many cafés that lined the open space. It was perfect for watching the front doors of the church.

Council members had gone inside regularly since I'd arrived, but I'd yet to see Ubhan walk in. Considering he was a night owl, he might not have left last night.

Quinn strolled up, looking casual and perfect for a day out. He grinned when he saw me and sat down. "So glad you could join me for our date."

I gave him a cheeky smile. "Wouldn't miss it."

Quinn, Grey, and I were planning to break into Ubhan's office this morning while Eve stayed behind to care for Mac and Seraphia. Since Grey wasn't the type to enjoy a morning coffee on the square—it would draw attention if he sat around like a normal person—Quinn and I were pretending to be on a date.

Not that anyone was looking that closely at us. But Grey could hear us through our comms charms, and I had a feeling that Quinn would flirt with me just to annoy him. He didn't realize the truth of our dire situation, and I wasn't about to tell him.

"The coffee is excellent," I said to him as the waitress approached. "My cappuccino is the best I've had in town."

It was a lie, but the waitress smiled, as I'd hoped she would. Better to have her on our side. Quinn placed his order for the same. After she'd left, I gave him a quick update of what I'd seen.

As soon as the visitor from Glasgow arrived—in a kilt, according to Miranda's sources—we were going to make our move.

The waitress returned with Quinn's coffee, and he

thanked her before she left. Instead of drinking it, however, he pressed his fingertips to his comms charm to turn it off and nodded for me to do the same.

I frowned at him, knowing that Grey wouldn't be able to hear us, but did as he asked. "What is it?"

"Are you sure about this thing with the Devil you have going?" His voice was pitched low enough that no one else could hear.

"What do you mean?"

"I've seen the way he looks at you, and Carrow—he's dangerous. Too dangerous."

"I know he is. But he's not a threat to me." To himself, maybe, because I had a feeling that he would walk right into hell to spare me, but he was not dangerous to me.

Quinn frowned. "I don't like it."

I scowled at him.

He raised his hands in apology. "But it's not my place to have an opinion on it, I get it. I like you, Carrow, and I don't want anything to happen to you."

A bit of warmth pushed aside most of the annoyance. "I get it, Quinn. And thank you for caring. I understand that Grey has a certain...reputation around town. But I'm fine."

He nodded and turned to the church. "Let's keep a lookout."

"Great." I uncovered my comms charm.

Grey's voice drifted out, quiet yet concerned. "Is everything all right? The line died."

"Everything is fine," I said.

A slight frown tightened Quinn's lips, but he said nothing as he gazed at the fire-darkened exterior of Black Church. The structure looked ominous against the bright blue sky.

I spotted a man wearing a kilt striding toward the front doors. "He's here," I murmured, but loudly enough for Grey to hear. "Meet you soon."

Quinn paid for our coffees, and I stood, grabbing the bag full of potion bombs that Eve had given me. We left holding hands for good measure. I assumed no one gave a damn about Quinn or me, but you never knew who might be watching.

We strolled along the edge of the square, and I gazed into shop windows as if interested in the wares. Slowly, we made our way closer to Black Church and ducked into a narrow side street. I tried to make it look like I was pulling Quinn in to make out with him, but I had no idea if the effect worked.

From the scowl on Grey's face, it was at least somewhat effective. The vampire stood in the shadows of a small intersecting alley, still as a statue and dressed in simple black tactical wear that would make running and fighting easy.

Quinn removed three small vials from his pocket

and handed them around. "Drink these. Eve made them. They'll make it so that it's difficult for anyone who sees us to remember our faces. But it only works for short encounters, so if you have a conversation, it won't work."

"Thanks." I swigged it back, appreciatively. It would be a big help with any admin staff or guards that we came across in the halls.

"Come," Grey said. "My contact is waiting."

Though we'd broken into Black Church through the dwarves' underground tunnels last time, we didn't have that option now. The Council had blocked off that secret entrance into their dungeons.

We followed Grey down the side streets, working our way to the back of Black Church. He'd said he had a contact in the kitchens, and they were going to let us in the back.

A young man stood outside, smoking a cigarette as he leaned against the brick wall. His apron was scattered with flour, and his face was sullen.

"This guy?" I asked skeptically.

"He wants out," Grey said.

"Out?"

"Out of Guild City. After he does this for us, he's going to make himself scarce for a while."

"The perfect candidate, then." It made sense. If the Council found out that he'd sneaked us in, he'd end up in jail.

The back street was empty, so we hurried toward the

kid. He gave the Devil a look, then turned and pressed his hand to the door. Magic sparked around his palm, and he pulled it open, the cigarette hanging from his mouth as he held out his free hand to Grey.

As Grey strode through the door, he passed the kid a thick envelope—cash, no doubt—and our accomplice grinned.

I nodded at him and walked through, Quinn bringing up the rear. The door shut quietly behind us, and I could imagine the kitchen boy already high-tailing it for one of the gates at the edge of town. I hoped he had a damned good time wherever he ran off to.

The hallway in which we stood was quiet and dark.

"The kitchens are near here," Grey murmured. "They keep a staff since so many Council members spend all day in their offices."

I shifted the bag over my shoulder, reaching inside for a stunner. The smooth glass ball fit perfectly in my hand as I gripped it loosely.

Grey met my eyes and raised an eyebrow.

I grinned. "Just in case."

"You know the way to Ubhan's office?" Quinn asked.

"Yes," Grey said. "We'll drop you at the main meeting room on the way."

"Perfect." Quinn nodded. He was going to deploy an alarm on the doors that would alert us when the meeting was out.

As we slipped silently through the halls, the thrill of the chase raced through my veins.

We were going to get him.

I didn't know how Ubhan was involved, but he was. And there were answers here.

Our footsteps were silent as we hurried down the hall, three shadows that stuck close to the wall. Grey led the way, as he knew the layout well, and I took the middle. Behind me, Quinn moved with lethal grace, making it easy to imagine him as a leopard.

Faint footsteps sounded up ahead, and I peered around Grey's shoulder. A hallway joined with our current one. Someone was headed in our direction. My heart rate jumped, and I tightened my grip on my stunner bomb, ready to throw it.

A guard dressed in black tactical wear like Grey's appeared in the intersection. Shock flashed across the man's face when he spotted us.

"Intruders. You shouldn't be back here." He raised his hand, magic sparking around his palm, and hurled the blast at us.

Grey lunged forward, dodging the blast and punching the guard in the face.

The man's head snapped back, and he staggered. Grey grabbed him before he fell, hauling him upright, but the man sagged, unconscious.

"Nice hit," Quinn said, sounding impressed.

"Thanks. Carrow, can you get his belt?"

I quickly unhooked it, and Grey turned him around. Wrapping the guard's wrists together, I bound them tightly behind his back. Then I knelt and untied his shoelaces, binding his ankles together in a triple knot he couldn't reach even if he tried. Last, I took the knife Quinn handed me and used it to tear off a strip of his shirt to gag him.

"There's a closet here." Quinn held open the door he'd found, and Grey stuffed the unconscious body inside.

The whole ordeal had taken less than a minute, and we were on our way once more.

When we reached the main foyer that led toward the meeting room, Quinn peeled off. "Listen for the alarm," he said, his gaze on mine. "And good luck."

"You, too. Get out of here after you've deployed it. Don't get caught without backup."

He nodded, then looked at Grey. "Take care of her."

I raised my eyebrows. "How about we take care of each other?"

Quinn grinned. "Sure."

"Boys." I shook my head as he hurried toward the doors he planned to set with a trigger-based alarm.

"This way." Grey's voice was low as he led me down another hall and up a wide staircase to the next floor. "I believe his office is over here."

There was no one about as we walked, but I kept my senses on high alert. Tension hung heavy in the air as we moved through the old stone corridors, our footsteps silent on the wide wooden floorboards. Tapestries and dim sconces dotted the walls, giving the place an ancient feel.

At the end of the hall, we reached a wide door marked with Ubhan's name. The script was gold and gaudy, and I raised an eyebrow. "That's very appropriate for him."

Grey's lips twitched as he inspected the door, hovering his hands over the wood. Intricate carvings decorated the stone surrounding the frame. I'd bet my last adult juice box there was a spell on this door.

"It's enchanted," Grey confirmed. "Protective spells to lock it."

"Good thing I came prepared." I reached into the bag Eve had packed for me and withdrew a small silver stone, a spell reader. Hopefully, it would give us an idea of what protected his office.

Carefully, I ran it over the door, holding it close to the wood but not so close that it touched. When I ran it past the carved stones around the door jam, it vibrated slightly. I pointed to the spot. "The enchantment is there."

"Can that stone break the protection charm?"

"Eve said that it can break some charms, but not all. This seems to be too strong." I glanced down the hall, my heart racing faster. We were exposed. Any second, someone might walk by.

"The carvings on the stones say something, but I can't decipher it," Grey said.

"Same." There were twelve of them, each about ten centimeters square, positioned at regular intervals around the door. I pressed my fingertips to one, calling on my magic. *How do we open you?*

I had a vision of myself stepping on one of the stones set into the floor in front of the door, but nothing about the carved stones around the door jam. They were important, though. I could feel it.

I withdrew my hand. "Let's ask the others."

I took my phone from my pocket and snapped a picture, then texted it to Eve with a note that said:

The protective spell on Ubhan's door. Any idea how we get in?

My phone buzzed with a reply about thirty seconds later:

Seraphia says they are the months of the year, written in Sanskrit. Press them in order.

.   .   .

The end of the text included the translations for the months.

"Thank fates we have a friend who's a librarian." I raised my hand, ready to press the stone.

"Wait." Grey gripped my shoulder gently. "Ancient sorcerers used to start the year in June. They don't anymore, but he may have done it that way."

I nodded, moving my hand toward June. One after the other, I pressed the stones, feeling them vibrate beneath my touch. The last one pulsed hardest, and the door began to glow.

Grey reached for it, twisting the knob, but nothing happened. The vibration increased.

"An alarm," Grey said. "We're missing part of the spell."

Shit.

Heart racing, I studied the door, searching for the clue. The trembling became a loud hum that grew, climbing to a shriek.

My gaze went to a spot on the floor. The stones looked unassuming, but one of them matched what I'd seen in my vision.

I pressed my foot on it, hard.

The stone depressed, and the alarm stopped.

I sagged, relief chilling my skin.

Grey tried the door again, and this time, it opened easily. We slipped inside, and he closed the door behind us. I leaned against the wood, panting.

"Did you hear the alarm?" Grey spoke quietly into his comms charm.

"No, you're good," Quinn responded. "I've just deployed the alarms on these doors. Your comms charm will ping when they are tripped."

"Good," I said. "Get out of there."

"See you on the outside," he replied. "Call for backup if you need it."

We cut the connection, and I stared at the office.

It was filled to the brim with books and papers. Crowded shelves climbed to the ceiling fifteen feet above us.

"There have to be thousands of them," I said. "Have you been in here before?"

"No," said Grey. "He doesn't let anyone in."

Three huge tables and a massive desk were covered in papers, as if a mad scientist were hard at work.

At the edges of the room, a faint mist began to seep from beneath the walls. "What's that?"

Grey frowned. "I've never seen the like."

The mist moved quickly, filling the room. I breathed it in, unable to help myself.

My mind fogged, and my thoughts and memory became fractured.

Why were we here?

Mac.

"It's a mind-numbing spell," Grey said.

My thoughts tumbled over themselves as I tried to

figure out what was going on and how to fix it. But I was so slow. So tired.

The weight of my potion bag pulled at my shoulder, and an idea pushed through the haze that clouded my mind.

Hadn't Eve given me something that could help with spells like this?

Frantic, I scrambled in my bag for the tiny star-shaped bottle she'd shown me. My fingers closed around it. Opening the bottle with trembling hands, I took a small sip, then passed it off to Grey. "It should clear your mind."

It was already working on me, giving me a magical resistance to the mist that still hung heavy in the air. My thoughts cleared, and I remembered why we were there.

Grey drank some of the potion, and his gaze sharpened. "That worked well."

"Let's search the room." I took a staggering step. Was I tired, or was another spell at work?

Impossible to say.

Grey and I quickly rifled through the papers. I scanned documents and books, trying to keep my power in check so my mind wouldn't become polluted by too many unrelated visions.

Ubhan had varied interests, most of which seemed to be focused on different parts of history. Many of the documents were related to the rules and regulations of the city and the Council. He was a rule follower through and through, as all sorcerers tended to be.

"I think I may have found something," Grey said.

I hurried toward him, my eyes riveted to the ancient, yellowed papers in his hands. "What is it?"

"They appear to be redacted minutes from a Council meeting a few hundred years ago. From the Council of 1642, specifically."

"After your time."

"Yes. I'd left by then."

"Why is he so interested in redacted minutes?"

"Because the Council doesn't redact minutes. At least, we didn't when I was on it. To my knowledge, they still don't."

"Ubhan wouldn't like that. He's a big fan of the rules."

"Sorcerers." Grey shook his head and looked back at the paper. His brow creased. "He either wanted to get to the bottom of the redacted minutes or he had something to do with it."

"My bet is on the latter." I ran my gaze over the writing, noting the parts that were heavily blacked out. "What decision was the Council trying to hide?"

"I can't tell. Someone's marked through the text."

On the desk, there were more collections of minutes. Black lines crossed through some of the lines on them as well. I reached out to touch one, calling upon my gift.

What do you hide?

I'd hoped the blacked-out words would appear in my mind, but I was out of luck.

Instead, an image appeared—an interior stone wall and wooden floor. Near the floor, one of the stones glowed, calling to me. I turned, feeling the pull from behind me. One of the stones in the wall caught my attention. There, near the floor.

I walked toward it, my movements oddly sluggish, but I was too enraptured by the wall in front of me to care. I reached it, knelt, and pried at the stone. It budged slightly. I pulled harder, and the stone came out. A small cubbyhole appeared.

"What's in there?" Grey hunkered down beside me.

I reached inside the dark space, anticipation streaking through me. My fingertips touched paper, and I pulled out a pile of pages that had been bound together.

A Most Elucidating History of Guild City.

The title of the book was scrawled across the top of the first page. I looked at Grey, grinning. "It's the pages that were torn from the book."

I untied the bundle and began to read, shock racing through me.

"Oh my God..." I murmured.

"Another guild." Surprise sounded in Grey's voice. "That's the memory that was taken from me."

"The Shadow Guild." At the words, recognition

flared within me. "A guild for all those who don't fit into the others. For the misfits and the strange ones."

Like me.

But it had been erased from history.

The comms charm around my neck buzzed, a harsh alarm sounding.

"The meeting is out." Grey stood, his movements oddly slow. "We need to go."

I struggled to my feet. It was hard to walk. The air in the room was viscous and thick, trapping us. I glanced at Grey. His brow was creased in concentration.

"What's wrong?" I asked. "Why can't we move?"

"It's a spell of some sort." He frowned and tried to force his body toward the door. "We triggered it at some point. Perhaps when we touched the papers."

I pushed against the sludgy air but couldn't get more than a few inches. The alarm continued to sound from around my neck, the seconds ticking down.

Ubhan would be here any moment.

16

THE DEVIL

Ubhan's spell held us tight, making it nearly impossible to move. Every step took a minute, like we were pushing our way through a solid substance.

The door swung open, and Ubhan appeared.

At the sight of us, rage lit his eyes. "*What* are you doing here?"

I met his gaze and imbued my voice with all of my power. "Stop the spell that binds us. *Immediately.*"

Deep lines bracketed his mouth as he fought my command, but, finally, he acquiesced. He waved his hand and muttered an unidentifiable word. The spell snapped, and suddenly, I was able to move.

I drew in a steadying breath, reining in my temper, and spoke sharply. "Sit."

He moved woodenly to a chair. "I warn you, guards are coming."

It was what we'd wanted to avoid—along with Ubhan's knowledge of our theft—but it could be dealt with. "Wait there, and do not say a word."

My magic drifted toward him. It forced him to comply, but it couldn't quell his rage. Even if we made it out of here with the information we sought, I'd made him an enemy.

Carrow put the torn-out pages of the book in her bag and went to the office door. She flattened against the wall, hidden from whomever entered. I joined her, lining up on the other side.

We made eye contact.

"I'll take the first," I whispered.

She nodded, reaching into her bag for a potion bomb.

A guard rushed in. I tripped him, yanked him up, and punched him hard in the jaw. His head snapped back, and he collapsed, unconscious.

I spun around, spotting Carrow as she hurled a potion bomb at the next guard. The brilliant red orb exploded against a female shifter's chest, soaking her in gleaming liquid. Her eyes rolled back in her head, and she went down like a sack of rocks, landing with a thud.

Two more men rushed in. One of them reached for the comms charm at his neck. I lunged at him and snatched the charm off. He swung at me, landing a blow to my cheek. I saw stars, and my head spun, but I shook off my dizziness and kicked him in the midsection. He crashed into a bookcase. The wooden shelves rattled, and dozens of books tumbled off. Behind me, Ubhan made a pained noise.

Carrow took out the other guard with a potion bomb while I reached for the man buried beneath the pile of books. I dragged him upright and delivered a punch that knocked him out.

Carrow peered around the edge of the door. "No more are coming."

"They'll come when these four don't report back," Ubhan said. "Then you'll regret this."

"Then we'd better be quick," I said.

Together, Carrow and I bound the fallen guards with their shoelaces and belts.

I turned to Ubhan. "We'd hoped to not have to do it this way."

"I'll have your head for this," Ubhan spat. "Hers, too."

I didn't know how deep this cover-up went—whether it would be a battle with Ubhan or the entire council—but we'd figure it out. "You're hardly in a position to make threats."

Carrow pulled the book's pages out of her bag. "Why were you hiding these in the wall?"

Confusion flickered in his eyes. "The wall?"

She pointed to the section of wall that was still missing a stone. "I found the missing pages of *A Most Elucidating History of Guild City* in there. And on your desk, we found the redacted meeting notes from when the Council made the decision to hide the Shadow Guild."

"What the bloody hell are you talking about?" His gaze moved to his desk. "What is the Shadow Guild?"

"You can't tell me you're unfamiliar with all of this." I spoke smoothly, imbuing my voice with my power. "What do you know, Ubhan? What have you done?"

His lips twisted. "I've read the redacted meeting notes—what I can see of them, at least. I discovered them while researching the history of the Council and found it to be highly suspect that they would redact their notes. We do not engage in such behavior, as you know."

I nodded. "Continue."

"I knew the Council of 1642 was trying to hide something, which is *also* highly unusual and suspect." Irritation flickered in his eyes. Ubhan *hated* breaking the rules. "It was long ago, but I wanted to get to the bottom of it. So I've been researching."

"And part of that research involved stealing the pages from *A Most Elucidating History of Guild City?*" Carrow asked.

"I don't know what the bloody hell that is."

"I found them in your wall." She held up the papers.

"For your information, I am not the only person who has ever occupied this office." His eyes flashed. "You slight my honor when you suggest I would deface a history book and hide the pages here."

I studied his features, looking for the truth. For the lie.

I hated to think he might be innocent, but it seemed more and more likely. Ubhan was a pain in the arse and a miserable bastard, but he was a true stickler for the rules. And my power was compelling him to tell the truth.

Carrow flicked through the pages in her hand. "So you knew nothing of the Shadow Guild or the fact that the Council of 1642 voted to disband it and hide it from history, making all magical misfits in Guild City outlaws?"

"No, I knew nothing of the sort. Just that they were hiding something by redacting the meeting notes."

"Who had this office in 1642?" I asked.

Ubhan frowned, thinking back. "That would have been Councilor Rasla."

"Of course." Carrow shook her head. "That bastard made it a rule that everyone has to join a guild and control their signatures. He couldn't stand those who were different, those who joined the Shadow Guild, so he hid it with his curse and struck it from the history books and your memories."

"That's quite the tale," Ubhan said.

"It's true," Carrow said. "And we don't know the whole of it yet, but we will."

I studied him, debating what to do. Our time was limited here, after all. "Have you told us everything you know?"

"Yes."

I frowned. His eyes looked weaselly. I might not like him, but Ubhan was smart. "What other relevant documents do you have?"

His scowled deepened.

Yes, I'd hit the nail on the head. "Hand them over, and we'll call it good between us."

"After this invasion, it will *never* be good between us."

"We've uncovered the corruption you sought to reveal yourself, so we'll consider it even."

We'd had the same agenda, but he would still hate us. I'd have to ensure Carrow's safety before the curse took me to hell. He didn't have the power to bother me, but I couldn't leave her unprotected.

Ubhan's lips twisted, and his gaze moved to the table on his left. "There is a small leather book on that table. Given what you've said about Councilor Rasla, I think it will be of use to you. It is his personal diary."

My brows rose. "How did you find that?"

"Secured beneath the desk by a special adhesive."

"He was all about hiding things around this office, wasn't he?" Carrow asked.

"He died quite suddenly in 1643," Ubhan said. "It seems that he didn't have time to clean the office."

"All the better for us." She went to the table and retrieved the book, then turned back to him. "Is there anything else?"

"Not that I know of."

A disembodied voice came from a comms charm around a fallen guard's neck.

"It's time to leave." I looked at Ubhan. "Stay seated there for ten minutes. Afterward, I suggest you not give us any trouble over this, or it will look like you support Rasla's actions."

Ubhan glared. "I'd never support such a thing."

"Good. Then we are on the same side." Carrow grinned and strode toward the door.

I followed her, and we made our way quickly through the halls. Near the stairs, we passed a reedy-looking man I recognized. He was an assistant to one of the council members, but he didn't do more than glance at us.

"Are you sure he'll stay put?" Carrow asked as we began to descend the stairs.

"Ubhan? Yes, for the ten minutes, at least. After that, my hold won't work on him."

She nodded. "We'll be across town by then. Let's go

to my place to check on Mac and Seraphia. We can read the diary there."

"Excellent plan."

Together, we hurried across Guild City. Carrow clutched the bag containing the books and papers, a deep frown on her face. "I really hope there's a cure for Mac and Seraphia in here."

"We'll find it. I promise."

She looked up at me, eyes wide. "We haven't even figured out how to fix *us,* much less them."

She had a point.

We reached her place a few minutes later, and she took the stairs two at a time. The door to Mac's flat was slightly ajar, and she ducked inside.

"How are you feeling?" she asked.

I joined her in the flat. Mac and Seraphia were on the couch, looking pale and wan. Eve appeared in the kitchen doorway. Her face was streaked with something purple.

"Fine," Mac said.

"I'm working on a strength potion to give them," Eve said. "But we need a cure. Soon."

"This will sound strange," Seraphia said. "But I feel like the building is pulling at me. Like I want to return to it."

"Same," Mac said.

"Yes," Carrow frowned. "It's odd, but I feel it too." She looked at me. "Do you?"

"I feel nothing."

"Well, we've got more clues." Carrow held up the book and pulled the pages out of her bag. She handed off the pages to Seraphia.

The librarian took them, interest gleaming in her eyes. "Where were they?"

Carrow sat in the chair near the window and relayed our adventures.

"There was another guild in town?" Shock shone in Mac's eyes. "The Shadow Guild, and none of us even knew about it?"

"It seems so," Carrow said. "And I don't think the building is evil. It's the curse that Councilor Rasla put on the place to hide it."

"And to kill the members," I said.

Carrow's gaze flashed to me, shock in their depths. "What?"

"It's the only way it could have stayed a secret," I said. "If we read his diary, I imagine we will find record of that. Otherwise, what would have happened to them once their tower was gone? Perhaps he erased some of their memories and evicted them from town, but it's just as likely the curse on the building killed them."

As it might kill Mac and Seraphia. I didn't say the words, but Carrow and the others were too clever not to intuit what was left unsaid.

"Does that mean I'm meant to belong to the Shadow Guild?" Mac asked.

"But you have a guild," Carrow said.

"I never fit in well." Mac shrugged. "One of the reasons I live here instead of there."

"I don't fit particularly well in mine, either," Seraphia added.

"This is insane," said Carrow.

"It could still be true," I said.

"But I wasn't cursed," she said. "And I'm currently the biggest misfit in town."

Mac leaned forward. "But the way your eyes glow, you're definitely connected to it. Just because you don't feel the effects of the curse doesn't mean you aren't part of it."

Carrow opened the tiny diary in her lap. "I'm going to get to the bottom of this. We've partially broken that curse. We need to finish the job. Then we'll have time to figure it out."

Seraphia flipped through the papers on her lap, handing some off to Mac. As they began to search the text, the sky darkened abruptly.

Carrow looked up, a frown creasing her brow. "That's weird. It's not even close to dusk."

Energy surged on the air, and thunder rumbled.

"That's even weirder," Mac said.

Wind began to howl, and the air prickled ominously, pulling from the direction of the Shadow Guild tower.

"Something is wrong." Eve walked to the window, and the others stood.

I joined her, looking out into the eerily dark sky. Dusk appeared to have fallen, and lightning exploded against the blackness.

"I'm going to check the tower," Eve said.

She spread her sparkling wings and launched herself off the windowsill and into the sky, flying in the direction of the tower on the other side of town.

Eve wasn't gone long. She flew back through the window, her eyes wide. "It's coming from the tower. We need to get over there."

Mac spoke into her comms charm. "Quinn? Meet us at the new tower. Bring any shifters you can get. We might need backup."

"Time, I need time," Carrow muttered. "There's something in this book. I feel it."

"Read and walk," Seraphia said.

Carrow nodded, her gaze on the book. Eve strode into the kitchen with a bag over one shoulder and two vials, one in each hand. She gave them to Mac and Seraphia, who gulped them down.

"What you really need is rest," Eve said.

"So do you." Mac looked her over. "You're pale."

"We're all pale, and we all feel like shit," Seraphia said. "Now, come on. Let's go win this fight."

My brows rose. There was more to the little librarian than first met the eye.

Eve gave Seraphia the bag. "That's full of potion bombs. Most are meant to kill, so be careful with them."

"Thank you." Seraphia looped it over her shoulder.

The four of us hurried down the stairs, Carrow bringing up the rear as she kept her nose buried in the book. I walked in front of her, close enough to catch her in case she tripped.

When we reached the street, Eve launched herself into the air once more and looked back at us. "I'm going to get a head start."

"Be careful," Mac said. "That lightning looks bad."

Eve kept low, flying just below the rooftops.

We pushed our way through the streets, which were crowded with people staring up at the strangely dark sky. The wind whipped more strongly, coming from the direction of the Shadow Guild tower.

"Getting any clues there, Carrow?" Mac asked.

"Maybe." Her eyes raced over the pages as she flipped through them. "There's got to be something about this."

We had nearly reached the narrow alley that led to the courtyard in front of the tower when Carrow yelped, "I found it!"

"What is it?" Seraphia asked.

"When the spell on the tower is threatened by the return of the guild members, Councilor Rasla will rise one last time to protect it."

"Guild members?" Mac said. "That has to be us."

Carrow nodded. "It says they will be led by one with

strange and deadly magic. It is her arrival that instigates it all."

"That's you," Mac said. "It has to be."

Carrow frowned, her eyes still racing over the page. "The disturbed magic will reinvigorate him for a short time. He will be powerful, so powerful that he can ensure his agenda once again."

"Killing all of us," Mac said. "Because I'm pretty sure that's his goal."

"And hiding the Shadow Guild once more," Seraphia said.

"We won't let him." Carrow snapped the book shut.

We reached the alley. I led the way, sprinting through the narrow space. It had become a wind tunnel. I forced my way through, pushing against the gale.

The courtyard in front of the Shadow Guild tower was chaos. Lightning struck overhead, thunder booming every few seconds. The ferocious wind roared and whipped the dead leaves in a cyclone.

Magic pulsed, oily and evil. It came from the statue at the center of the courtyard.

The others joined me, and Eve landed at our side.

As if it had been waiting for us, the magic pulsed once more, so hard that it popped my ears like we'd changed elevation.

"What's happening?" Mac shouted. "The magic is changing!"

The statue of Councilor Rasla exploded with a deafening boom. Shards of stone bombarded us, and we ducked against the wall to protect our faces. I wrapped myself around Carrow and Mac, who stood closest. The stone sliced through my back and arms, and Carrow hissed in pain.

As soon as it stopped, we whirled around.

The statue was gone. In its place stood a man formed of thick smoke instead of muscle and bone. Power radiated from him, chilling me to my core.

17

CARROW

Fear shivered through me when I saw the man. If black holes were human-shaped, they would look like him. When he moved, it was with a sinuous, snakelike motion.

Though he had no eyes, I could feel his gaze upon me. His voice was cold and smooth, evil incarnate. "So, *you* are the cause of all this trouble."

I drew in a deep breath. "You'll never succeed, Rasla."

His laughter made the hair stand up on my arms.

He turned his attention to Grey. "Ah, Devil. You live yet, in your fashion. Did you like what I did with your memory?"

"It was a delight." The ice in Grey's voice rivaled that of Rasla's.

My mind raced as I watched the two of them. Rasla's personal diary had crowed about his plans and accomplishments, but it had provided no clues about his weaknesses or how to beat him.

I touched my comms charm and whispered into it, hoping to reach Quinn.

"Yes?" His voice was quiet.

"Come around from the side, along the wall. Not through the alley. We'll surround him."

"Be there in one minute. I've got four shifters for backup. More on the way."

We needed to buy time, but behind Rasla, the ramshackle tower began to pulse with dark magic. The walls seemed to expand and contract. The pressure in the air changed, making me lightheaded. The wind shrieked louder, and a sense of foreboding crashed over me.

The windows in the building shattered with a bang, exploding outward. I ducked and covered my head, hissing as glass rained down, cutting into my flesh.

When it stopped, I looked up. Midnight smoke seeped out of the gaping windows, reeking of decay and death. It twisted through the grass, moving as quickly and sinuously as snakes.

The coils of dark smoke wrapped around my ankles, then Eve's. It went for Mac and Seraphia last.

Behind Rasla, Quinn and four shifters appeared, entering the courtyard from the other side. The black smoke raced toward them, wrapping around Quinn's ankles as well.

I gasped as the oily slickness shot through me. The sensation quickly faded, but Eve and Quinn doubled over, retching. Mac and Seraphia stumbled but didn't appear to be as hard hit as the others.

What the hell was going on?

"It has already started!" Rasla crowed. "My magic grows, and my curse knows how to find outcasts like you. The worst manner of villains. You'll be gone soon, along with your precious Shadow Guild, once and for all."

No.

This was my home. I could feel it. My gift could feel it. The very air I breathed in this abandoned part of town screamed that I needed to protect this place from him.

A shard of window glass gleamed at my feet. I reached for it, letting my magic flow through me.

How can I stop him? How can I protect you?

The answers came quickly, as if my gift knew there was no time to spare.

I was the one he'd written about in his journal. The one who would arrive and bring back the Shadow Guild.

Somehow, we were linked.

I had the power to stop him. It was why my eyes glowed neon green, why the curse didn't debilitate me like it had Mac and Seraphia.

The knowledge—the power—pulsed inside me, drawing me to him. I had to touch him, to use my magic to destroy him. Then I could save the tower.

I dropped the shard of glass, the answers whirling inside my mind.

Grey stepped forward, drawing a sword from the ether. Rasla raised his hands above his head, and the smoke that hovered over the ground rose, forming creatures of swirling black glass held together by smoke. They were shaped like humans, but every part of their bodies was a weapon.

A dozen figures formed a protective circle around Rasla. He laughed, the sound eerie against the crack of thunder.

"Obsidia demons," Mac said. "Deadly bastards."

"I need to get to him." I reached into the bag Eve had given me, drawing out a potion bomb. "I can stop him."

Grey started forward, so fast he was a blur. He clashed with one of the Obsidia, his blade slicing through an arm. The limb dropped off, but the creature swiped out with his other, delivering four deep gashes to Grey's chest.

Across the square, the shifters roared. Instead of transforming into their animal forms, they drew swords from the ether and charged.

It was wise. Shifters fought with teeth and claws, but the Obsidia could tear them apart if they made contact.

Eve launched herself into the air, her wings carrying her high as she raised her hands and shot a blast of lightning at one of the Obsidia. The creature exploded in a burst of glittery, pulverized glass.

At my side, Mac raised her blade and staggered forward. Seraphia did the same, pulling a wicked looking dagger from the ether. She reached into the bag that Eve had given her and withdrew a potion bomb. She passed it to Mac before taking one for herself.

"Stay back here," I said. "You're too weak."

"We'll be dead if we lose," Mac said.

"Just keep your distance," I implored.

She nodded. "Be careful."

I sprinted toward the horde of Obsidia that stood between me and my target, hurling my potion bomb at one of them. It collided with the creature's chest, and the beast shattered into a thousand pieces.

The battle raged, glass and smoke flying. The monsters were deadly but brittle. They weren't particularly hard to kill, but one of their blows was devastating. As soon as our forces took out one of theirs, another would appear.

A pair of Obsidia sprinted for me, their eyeless faces turned toward mine. I yanked a potion bomb out of the bag and hurled it at the closest one. The beast exploded, but the second was already on me.

The Obsidia lashed out. Glass sliced into my arm and shoulder, and pain flared. I stumbled back, grabbing another potion bomb. I threw it at the creature, my aim true. The beast blasted apart.

Blood poured from my shoulder and bicep. I spun around, searching for the next threat. One of them lunged for me, and I ducked, narrowly avoiding a hit as pain burned in my arm. I dug out another potion bomb and chucked it in the face of my attacker. The creature shattered.

In the distance, Grey fought like a whirlwind, so fast that he was nearly a blur. His sword cut through the Obsidia with ease. Beheading them worked well, but there were so many. The shifters and my friends kept up the attack, but we were outnumbered three to one. My friends were covered in wounds, and blood stained the dirt around us.

I sprinted for Rasla. It was up to me to take him out. But another group of Obsidia cut me off, three of them advancing. Black glass glittered ominously within the smoke that held them together. I hurled my potion bomb at one, but the pain and blood loss had killed my aim. The bomb detonated at the creature's feet, and it leapt over, sprinting for me.

From the sky, Eve hit it with a blast of lightning, taking it down. There were still two more, though, and they were nearly on me. I plunged my hand into my bag, arm singing with pain. I drew out another bomb and managed to hit the second monster. It erupted in a burst of sparkling glass, but the third was on me in seconds, taking me to the ground.

As I fell, I caught sight of Mac going down, then a shifter.

There were just too many.

I thrashed and struggled, pain nearly blinding me as the beast wrapped its entire body around mine. It felt like falling into a pit of glass shards, thousands of cuts that gouged deep.

My blood poured onto the dirt, leeching out of me. Too fast. Too many cuts. Too deep.

Dying.

A roar sounded in the distance, and a second later, the monster on top of me was gone.

The pain remained, so strong and blinding that I could barely see.

Grey leaned over me. "Carrow," he said, terror in his voice, "can you hear me?"

I nodded, my head already foggy from wounds. I could barely think, but I knew one thing—the blow had been too much.

I was dying. We were losing. It was over. "We're...outnumbered."

"We're not," he said. "More shifters have come. Open your eyes."

I struggled to open my eyes, barely able to see the shifters behind him. There were over a dozen of them with shields and long swords. Screams and shouts sounded, and explosions of glass flew into the air as the shifters took out the Obsidia.

Eve's lightning lit the sky, and I caught sight of Mac and Seraphia out of the corner of my eye. They hurled potion bombs at any Obsidia who came close. Rasla was nowhere to be seen, but I could still feel his presence.

The battle continued to rage, but I was too weak to sit up.

"Take my blood." My voice was so faint that I wasn't sure he could hear me. "I won't make it, but you could. End the curse."

"Absolutely not." Fear echoed in his voice. Fear for me.

Cordelia appeared at my side, wringing her hands, her eyes worried.

Poor Cordelia. Who would buy her kebabs?

Cordelia tugged at Grey's sleeve. *Heal her.*

"I can't." Grey's voice broke slightly. "The curse has taken my healing ability."

"I'm dying, Grey. I can feel it."

I could see the truth in his eyes. It would take an enormously powerful healing charm to get me out of this, and with the battle raging...

If Eve had had one, she'd have put it in my pack.

It took all my strength to grip his arm. "Take my blood and save yourself."

"You're out of your mind with pain," he said.

He was right about that. I'd never been in such agony. It tore through me like fire. I could never come back from something like this.

"I'm not doing it," he said. "I don't want immortality. Not if it steals your life from you."

Stubborn man. "My life is already gone."

A figure appeared at our side, falling to his knees by my head.

I blinked up, confused. "Michael?"

The big man of unknown species stared down at me. The last time I'd seen him, we'd been waving at him from Xavier's canal boat.

I brought him, Cordelia said.

I blinked.

"You need to take this." Michael pulled a tiny vial out of a wrist cuff. "You don't have long."

"What is it?" Grey demanded.

"Powerful healing draft. Strongest one I've ever made." He uncorked it and held it over my lips. "Drink. Now."

I did as he said, gulping down the bitter liquid. Strength surged through my muscles, and I gasped. My vision cleared, and after a few moments, I was able to sit.

Shocked joy surged through me, and I looked between Cordelia and Michael.

"She was paying my chickens a visit when she

sensed you were in danger," Michael said. "She dragged me along."

"Thank you." I stumbled upright with Grey's help, taking in our surroundings.

The battle was slowing, but Mac was still on the ground. Two shifters as well. I spun back to Michael. "Will you help them? Please?"

He nodded and ran toward Mac.

The sounds of battle raged as I searched the darkness for Rasla. He'd retreated when we'd started to gain the advantage.

"He's by the tower." Grey pointed.

"I'm going for him." Magic surged inside me. The connection between us burned, strange and unholy. I needed to get rid of some of this power, shove it into him until he exploded. I was an atomic bomb ready to detonate.

I sprinted toward Rasla, and Grey joined me. "Let me. You were just wounded."

"It has to be me." My power pulsed inside me, drawing me toward him. Rage boiled in my veins.

Grey took out two Obsidia as we neared the sorcerer.

Dark magic pulsed around Rasla, and the tower that loomed at his back seethed with the same darkness. I was determined to drive it from Guild City. From the Shadow Guild tower. From my friends.

I could grab a potion bomb from my bag, but it would do no good. I was sure of it. The power was within *me*, the magic of Orion's Heart, and it needed to go somewhere. The atomic bomb feeling intensified.

Rasla saw me and charged with a roar. I hurled myself at him, grabbing tight to him as my magic erupted. His grip sliced at me, sending electric pain through my limbs, but I was stronger. My power blasted into Rasla. He shrieked, flailing backward.

Before my eyes, he turned to ash and blew away on the wind.

But the Shadow Guild tower still vibrated with dark magic. The curse was alive and well.

"Why didn't it work?" I cried.

The sounds of battle around us faded. The Obsidia had disappeared along with Rasla, but some of the dark magic remained, polluting the tower in front of us.

It called to me, singing a siren song that I couldn't resist. Desperate, I hurried to a window on the first floor and scrambled through it, cutting my hands on the glass shards. I barely registered the pain.

"Wait up!" Mac's voice sounded from behind me.

But I was already inside. Grey followed. We stood in a large, empty room that looked like it had housed only rats for the last four hundred years. Dust and barren stone walls echoed with Rasla's evil curse.

Mac climbed in behind me, then Seraphia, Quinn, and Eve.

"I feel drawn here," Quinn said.

"Me, too." Eve stepped deeper into the tower.

"I feel better." Mac's voice had brightened. "The curse. I don't feel it as much."

"Neither do I," Eve said.

"We had to come in here," Mac said.

"It's still polluted, though," I murmured. I could feel it like I could feel the pull of gravity. "His stain is still on this place."

I walked forward, searching for the source of whatever called to me. An enormous fireplace beckoned from the far side of the room. A black gem was set into the stone mantle, gleaming dully with evil. My magic surged to the surface, and my palms itched to touch it.

"Your eyes are going wild again, mate," Mac said. "Neon green."

The black stone beckoned. When I pressed my palms against it,

I could feel the darkness inside the stone, inside the walls. But goodness, too. I pushed my magic into the gem, willing it to drive the curse away. Warmth flowed through my muscles and bones, along with a sense of rightness.

"It's working!" Mac said

I studied the stone in front of me, watching in awe as the gem began to turn dark red again. Slowly, the curse leeched from the walls, until the entire building felt...normal.

Exhausted, I pulled my hands away.

"Are you all right?" Grey gripped my shoulders, supporting me.

I leaned into him. "Yeah. Tired, but fine."

"Your eyes look normal again."

"I feel a lot more normal." Finally, I was able to look at Grey properly for the first time.

He looked like hell. Pale and covered in deep gashes, blood covering most of his clothing and skin. His eyes were dull from pain or blood loss. Or both.

Fear shot through me, and I spun. "Where is Michael? We need a healing potion for Grey."

"It's—"

"Not fine." I cut him off, knowing what he would say.

Michael shoved his huge body through the window and climbed inside. He took a potion from the cuff at his wrist and handed it to Grey, then disappeared again with some muttered words about seeing to the rest of the wounded.

Grey took the vial and drank it. The wounds knit themselves back together, and the color returned to his skin.

"How do you feel?" I asked.

"I'm all right. Don't worry about me."

How could I not, considering what I knew about us? About our fate?

I turned to Mac and Seraphia. "How do you feel?"

"One hundred percent." Mac frowned. "That was so

strange. Maybe I wasn't really cursed at all, like the Curse Diviner said. Maybe I just needed to come here."

"This place called to me," Seraphia said. "It was trying to bring us here. We felt the effects of Rasla's curse because this place was cursed. Not us."

I spun in a circle, looking around at the dusty old room. It looked like a castle. A freaking dragon should appear any minute.

"So, what does this mean?" I asked.

"I think you have a guild." Mac grinned widely. "And so do we."

18

The next day, I stood outside of Black Church with Mac, Seraphia, Quinn, Eve, and Grey. Cordelia sat at our feet, sunbathing on the stones. The morning was clear and bright. If I tried hard enough, I could pretend that yesterday had been a dream.

Only, it hadn't been.

We really did have a guild. And fortunately, no one on our side had died in the battle.

Now, we were waiting for our meeting with the Council.

And this time, I'd been the one to call the meeting. I looked at Mac.

"Ready to go tell them who's boss?" she said.

I nodded.

It's you. Cordelia grinned up at me.

"Shhh. We can't be so cocky about it," I said. "I'm still the new girl in town."

"Powerful new girl," Eve said. "You've only been here a couple weeks, and you're already a guild leader."

After the battle yesterday, they'd all voted. The Shadow Guild tower had made it clear that the five of us were meant to be members. We still had no idea how the practicalities were going to work out, but the Council would require a representative.

My friends had chosen me.

I didn't want the responsibility, but they wouldn't take no for an answer. I'd driven the curse from the tower. In their eyes, that made me qualified.

I looked at Grey, and he gave me a nod. "It'll be fine."

The thing with the Shadow Guild—yes. I'd see to it.

The thing with him?

I had no idea.

"Let's go," Mac said. "It's time."

The six of us strode into the church. Though Grey wasn't a member of our little guild, he was there as backup. I had no complaints.

In the main meeting room, the entire Council was waiting. When they caught sight of our group, they frowned. Only Cartimandua smiled. The leader of the Witches' Guild looked more intrigued than confused, and it reaffirmed my decision that she was my favorite.

"Carrow Burton, I thought you were here to reapply for a guild?" asked Mateo, the leader of the vampires. Leader of all except Grey, of course. He didn't join anything—not even my guild. "Why do you have these people with you?"

Something flickered in Ubhan's eyes. We hadn't spoken to him since we'd broken into his office, but he knew things had changed. The entire Council knew about the tower on the far side of town—it was hard to miss, now that it had appeared—but Grey's contacts said they were still uncertain about it.

I was here to enlighten them.

"As it happens, I have a guild." I gestured to my friends. "The Shadow Guild. The tower that has reappeared after a long absence is ours."

Murmurs rose, and several guild members stood. Ubhan stayed seated, his jaw set.

Cartimandua leaned forward. "You'll have to start from the beginning."

So I did, omitting the part about Orion's Heart. We still weren't entirely sure what role that power played, and it didn't matter right now. I even confessed to breaking into Ubhan's office, since I didn't want that hanging over my head.

I finished, and Nyla, the leader of the Mages' Guild, turned to Ubhan. "Is this true?"

He nodded. "What they found in my office, yes. Their interpretation? I have no idea."

"It's sounds true to me," Cartimandua said. "It makes sense that there would be a guild for those with unique powers. After all, we have members of our guilds who don't quite fit."

"This Rasla..." Nyla said. "He was a zealot?"

"As far as I could tell, yes," I said.

"He was," Grey said. "I knew him then, and I can confirm it. He'd likely have destroyed the tower altogether if it wouldn't have weakened the city's defenses to have an enormous hole in the wall."

"Yet, you defeated him," Cartimandua said. "And defended Guild City once again." She turned to look at her colleagues. "I vote to accept Carrow as a member of the Council and to fully reinstate the Shadow Guild."

There were some grumbles, primarily from Ubhan, but the vote went in our favor. When it was over, Cartimandua looked at me. "Congratulations. Now you get to come to meetings."

Damn.

Meetings were better than being evicted, though.

"Thank you," I said.

We turned to leave, and I caught Ubhan's eye. He glowered at me.

That was going to be a sticky relationship.

But as we walked out into the sun, it was impossible not to believe in fate. After all, it'd landed me here, amongst this crew of amazing, lovely supernaturals who were as strange and different as I was.

And now, we had a guild.

My friends were chattering away about plans for a party, but I only had eyes for Grey. He stood off to the side, his gaze on me.

He was thinking of our curse. It was written all over his face. And though the idea of it scared the hell out of me, the insanity of the last few days had proved that anything was possible.

Fate might have something terrible planned for us, but I wasn't going to let it come to pass. I'd saved the Shadow Guild. I'd save Grey, too.

I had to.

~~~

Thank you for reading! The adventure isn't over yet. Book four will be here in late July or early August :-D

THANK YOU!

THANK YOU FOR READING!

I hope you enjoyed reading this book as much as I enjoyed writing it. Reviews are *so* helpful to authors. I really appreciate all reviews, both positive and negative. If you want to leave one, you can do so at Amazon or GoodReads.

ACKNOWLEDGMENTS

Thank you, Ben, for everything. There would be no books without you.

Thank you to Jena O'Connor, Lexi George, and Ash Fitzsimmons for your excellent editing. The book is immensely better because of you!

Thank you to Orina Kafe for the beautiful cover art.

AUTHOR'S NOTE

Thank you so much for reading Dark Secrets! As always, there were a few historical tidbits that I wanted to share more about. The first is the Elizabethan gardens in front of the Mages' Coffeehouse. They are based off of the (much smaller) ones that are still preserved in Plymouth, England which were originally built in the 16th century.

The Mages' Coffeehouse was inspired by the coffeehouses that became popular in England for the first time in the 17th century. The beverage had been brought back to England by international travelers to Asia and was initially drunk for medicinal purposes. By the 17th century, it was popular in the same way it is today. The coffeehouses were places where people (men, primarily) met to discuss the news. Because no alcohol was served, they were generally thought to be places where more intellectual conversation could take place.

The first coffeehouse, established by a Jewish entrepreneur, was established in 1652 the town of Oxford (same as the famous university). Oxford was a particularly important town for the Establishment of coffeehouses. Though the first (called The Angel) is now gone, you can still visit Queen's Lane Coffee House, which was established in 1654 and is still running. It is considered to be the oldest continually operating coffeehouse in Europe.

Coffeehouses bore the nickname "penny universities". The name derives from the cost of admission (a penny) and the fact that they were hotbeds of intellectual discussion frequented by scholars and people from all walks of life. In a society with strictly divided social classes, coffeehouses were unique in the fact that all sorts of people mingled together. If you had the penny admission, you were welcomed in.

One of my favorite parts of *Dark Secrets* is the visit to Magic Side Chicago, where Carrow and Grey enlisted the help of Nevaeh Cross. For one, Magic Side is extremely cool. It's located offshore from South Side Chicago in the middle of Lake Michigan. Like Guild City, Magic Side is hidden from the larger human population. It's full of crazy cool magic set amongst skyscrapers and old warehouses inspired by Chicago's rich architectural heritage, ranging from elaborate Art

Deco facades to monumental Neo-Classical edifices. Future stories will return to Magic Side, providing an exciting chance to explore the magic and mystery inherent in many of Chicago's institutions, such as the Oriental Institute Museum, the Field Museum, and the Museum of Science and Industry - a relic from the 1893 World's Fair.

But most exciting of all...is that this isn't the last you'll see of Neveah Cross. She is the heroine of a new series I'm extremely excited about. I've co-written it with two of my best friends in the whole world—probably the only people I would trust to write in the Dragon's Gift World. They are both archaeologists like myself, so you can count on tons of fun adventures in the future. I'll keep you updated about the release date, but it's likely to be sometime in the early Autumn of 2020.

ABOUT LINSEY

Before becoming a writer, Linsey Hall was a nautical archaeologist who studied shipwrecks from Hawaii and the Yukon to the UK and the Mediterranean. She credits fantasy and historical romances with her love of history and her career as an archaeologist. After a decade of tromping around the globe in search of old bits of stuff that people left lying about, she settled down and started penning her own romance novels. Her Dragon's Gift series draws upon her love of history and the paranormal elements that she can't help but include.

COPYRIGHT

www.LinseyHall.com
https://www.facebook.com/LinseyHallAuthor